MOTHER BOX

and other tales

MOTHER BOX

and other tales

SARAH BLACKMAN

FC2
TUSCALOOSA

FC2 is an imprint of The University of Alabama Press

Book Design: Illinois State University's English Department's Publications
Unit; Director: Tara Reeser; Assistant Director: Steve Halle; Production
Assistant: Allie Maher
Cover Design: Lou Robinson
Typeface: Garamond

♾

The paper on which this book is printed meets the minimum requirements
of American National Standard for Information Sciences—Permanence of
Paper for Printed Library Materials, ANSI Z39.48–1984

Library of Congress Cataloging-in-Publication Data
Blackman, Sarah, 1980-
 [Short stories. Selections]
Mother Box and other tales / Sarah Blackman.
    pages cm
  ISBN 978-1-57366-174-4 (paperback : alk. paper) — ISBN 978-1-57366-
842-2 (ebook)
  I. Title.
PS3602.L325298M68 2013
813'.6—dc23
                              2013013567

To John and Helen
For both the theory and the practice

It was a summer night. Always it was summer in the womanish, childish, animal houseshape of God.

—Joy Williams

Two small dogs went to the wood,
new shoes on their feet.
Two small dogs going back home
having lost one of the shoes.
Two small dogs.

Two small dogs went to the wood,
spraining their ankles, turning their feet.
Two small dogs running home,
flour and husks up to their legs.
Two small dogs.

Two small dogs, their breasts are white.
Two small dogs with astonished eyes.
Two small dogs still staring out.
Two small dogs, "How are you tonight?"
Two small dogs.

—A Welsh children's song

Table of Contents

Mother Box

The people she knew, she had met under difficult circumstances. She wasn't the sort of girl who made friends—rather, she had contacts in the art world. She was a jazz pianist and a poet, a singer/songwriter, had taken up painting with acrylics and was practicing kinesthetic spiritualism. Also, she was taking a kind of medication that made her hair fall out along her part so that her part was becoming wider and whiter, the hair that remained on her head looking darker and coarser by contrast. Her mother called and wanted to know why her hair was falling out. "Why don't you *do* something about it?" her mother asked. "What kind of a person are you that this is alright?"

Of course, she was the sort of person who had a lot of secrets. Her secrets were how she understood it was herself and not, say, a peanut or a broken-bottomed chair. Listen, she was sort of a reprehensible figure. We knew it was cruel, but she didn't like us either and would sing wherever she went in piping notes like she was saying, "what WEEP? what WEEP?" over and over again. When we asked her what she was singing, she told us she was exercising her voice for an upcoming performance and then expressed one of her secrets which were stale and sodden, private examinations into the nature of the body suspended in a state of decay. Oh, oh! Our lives were so much worse now that she was in them. She had a dream about an onion, the she that was an onion. It was a secret she told us and that night we too had vegetative dreams, the fetid earth heaving above us, our best loved selves dissolving in the slip of gray rot.

Her mother called. She danced for us at a party, partially on a tabletop, partially on a stage she created by using stacks of the host's books for a backdrop. She invited us to notice the way she used only the muscles in her thighs to express the narrative. It was a story about a swan, a lucky oat cake, a boat and an evening sky. The apotheosis was conducted through a series of facial exercises that were guaranteed to keep her looking ten years younger than her chronological age. "My cellular age is only seventeen," she told us. Her mother called. She was invited to play the harp, a new accomplishment, at the wedding of a friend of one of our friends. The bride was enthusiastic. She was marrying on a golf course, beside a lake, in the country, at the end of a road lined with beeches. There was going to be a breakfast buffet. We were invited. We called our mothers. "This is not just some other tale of woe," we told our mothers, "this is non-quotidian, unparalleled, unable to be surmounted by ordinary measure." Our mothers are sometimes ferocious women, but all alive. Our mothers, at some point, guided our trembling fathers inside them and said it was okay, whatever they did next would be alright.

We thought this would be a sort of new beginning. We all moved to this town with some species of hope and had also started over a number of times before. At a party, we took the wrong door out of the bathroom and ended up in her bedroom. She had a tapestry tacked to her ceiling which was red and black and gold and filled with hundreds of tiny mirrors like the hundreds of eyes of a watchful peacock. It was horrible to see ourselves in the peacock eyes of her bedroom. We had ingested something. Someone knew what it was. The rest of the house was lit with blue and green lights like the loudest place there is under the ocean, but her room was dark and still as if the air couldn't move without a tremendous effort of will. One of her secrets was that she had almost been raped. It was when she was in college, a school on the coast that was nevertheless very far from the ocean. She wrote a one-act play about it and performed it wearing a giant papier-mâché onion with holes cut in the bottom for her legs. There was also a hole for her mouth, so she could speak, and during the play she would walk and speak, lost inside the enormous onion which had sat too long in its pantry, was sprouting a viridian green shoot which bobbed tremulously from its crest. "From my window I could smell the sea, salt spray, whale bone, smell the boom Boom BOOM of the waves broken against the shore, all this wreckage, all this birth," was one of the lines she shouted from inside the onion. We were in the audience, of course. We could not make ourselves just stay home. Every one of us had taken his hand and put it here, put it here. "Let's just get this over with," we had said, and then nothing else for a long time. Her mother called. "I made up the part about the ocean," she told us. "They were re-tarring the parking lot, so all I could really smell was asphalt. But everything else is true," she told us. "Everything else is witness."

Her mother called. She was performing body modifications, had split her tongue so it could lick and flit like a snake's tongue testing the air in the room. Her mother said, "Have you talked to the doctor yet? Have you put on some weight? Have you gotten a chromosomal scan? Have you examined your stool against a chart showing optimum consistency and shape?" Our mothers once came into our rooms at night and sat at the foot of the bed. We were reminded again how much bigger we were than our mothers by the only very small creak of the mattress beneath their weight. Our mothers wanted to know if we'd made any decisions, if we knew how fast the time was passing, if we thought we could wait forever. Did we think we could wait forever? We were supposed to have the ability to start all over. Just one more time. Some of us had painted all the walls of the house green as an onion shoot. Some of us put his hand here and said, "Tell that to your wife." Her mother called. At the wedding, she wore a dress made out of stinging nettles. She was so red with it her skin began to crack and weep a thin pink plasma. Of course, the bride was upset. From her room we had taken three little bottles of pills: blue pills, green pills, black pills with glossy coating. We mixed them together with some other things we had on our own. "Oops," we told our mothers.

The bride and groom had rented boats shaped like swans for the wedding party to arrive in. It was supposed to be a stately performance, at sunrise, across a lake gently heaving with large-mouth bass and catfish and some kinds of game trout imported from more wintery climes. The groom was a great outdoorsman. He was a young buck. She played a kind of polka-beat she said she had learned from a Transylvanian aroma-therapist she met while touring the European circuit. Then, she moved into an atonal dirge. Her skin wept so much from the nettles she left a thick pink slick on the chair when she took a break for lemonade and a turn at the breakfast buffet. Her mother called. We were all such good friends. We hated each other. We spun at the end of the dock and broke our teeth when we fell onto the rocky shore. Put your hand here. Put your hand here. None of the boats capsized, but the ladies were still discomfited. It had taken a long time to make it from once place to another. The day was steaming up from the lake bed. When the day reached the tops of the beeches it turned white, just like that. Her mother called. We had no shoes on. We had never had any shoes at all. Someone gave us a drink as pink as a berry, as sharp as a nettle. Nevertheless, at the end of the morning, they were legally obliged.

She set up a scaffold in front of the library. For awhile she hung there from a pair of gold hooks she inserted below her shoulder blades. She had bled herself pale, breasts flat against her ribs, hair receded almost to the tips of her ears where it flared like the shawl of an inky bird, the sort of bird that builds bowers. An architect bird we almost believed, at that moment, would take flight. Her mother called. One of her secrets was that she actually had been raped. She told us one night while we drank a juice made of nettles and dandelion leaves. We had turned over a new leaf, were cleansing ourselves by means of starvation and herbal unguents we rubbed on the soles of our feet so that everywhere we walked we left traces of our toxins. Our mothers thought we were taking things too far. "Who are you trying to prove this to?" our mothers asked. Meanwhile, some of us had gotten married. Our husbands had long torsos, blue veins, delicate hands and feet. We told them about the time we lay on her bed under the tapestry, what we saw, what we took. "He was a stranger," she said. "I left the door unlocked." She made a fetish doll with his features and carried it in her pocket everywhere she went. Her mother called. "What do you think this is doing to your father?" her mother wanted to know.

She was interested in the opposing impulses of Thanatos and Eros, Edo era pornographic scrolls, tribal dance, basket weaving, the intricate structures of the inner ear, past life revitalization, crystal theology, scribing through the entrails of freshly slaughtered beeves. Our husbands liked to turn us on our sides. They knew how to direct things so we did not have to see them, could only feel the hand on our hip, on our breast. Our husbands inside of us pushed past us and into a place that was suddenly white, just like that. We were like babies, wet and small. Our husbands wanted to know what we were thinking, why we were thinking, what we were doing, if we'd held on to any of those pills? "When it was over I asked him to marry me," she said. The doll had a wide mouth, always wet, always open. She touched the doll's face. Her mother called.

Listen, we knew it was cruel, but we had to have something. Our lives were not what we had been led to expect. There were things that had happened and kept happening over and over, like a hundred small mirrors in a dark room. She was interested in self-flagellation; she was documenting cases of scoliosis among teenage prostitutes; she had injected an ink in her eyes that turned the whites permanently black. Her mother called. For a terrible season we all dreamed we had given birth to an onion. We held it to our breasts, rubbing it back and forth on our breasts. Finally, we cut it up and made it into a soup. "This is the only chance you'll have," our mothers said. "I didn't believe it either, but it's true."

She told us so many things we couldn't keep track of what we didn't know about her. Our husbands might like us to have a baby. Our husbands think we should be mothers. Using an ancient Maori technique, she tattooed an exhaustive portrait of a man's back onto her front. The man's legs were spread over her legs, his back over her breasts, the back of his head with its thick brown hair inked over her face. The man was slimmer and taller than she and where his legs parted the pear droop of his sac obscured her pudenda. Her mother called. We said, "It's like she was raised by cardboard boxes. It's like she emits a ravenous void." Our mothers matured into beautiful women. They paint their nails a coral color, let their hair gray. When she talks her words come from the base of the man's brain, where his breathing is regulated, where his body remembers only itself. Oh, oh! From her room we took pills and a sense of darkness, a stack of letters she had addressed but never mailed. We wrote a letter to her mother. Our husbands put their fingers in our mouths and our ears. We asked them to. "Put your hand here," we said, but they were not always ours to command. Sometimes our husbands had the tusks of a boar or a single swan's wing. Sometimes their tongues were made of jade, their hands of thorns, their cocks trembling bundles of lilies still tightly furled.

Of course, we were right and hardly knew it. At the party, she danced for us. She left the doll in an empty space on the bookshelf as an audience. There were many delicious snack foods served. We were eating for two, had to go to the bathroom almost all the time. On her back she had tattooed a man's front. When she is coming, he goes with wide eyes, a simple expression. We clung to our husband's shirtfronts. We were delirious, dizzy. There was a knock at the door. She showed us how the narrative was contained by the gesture of her upper lip; she unrolled a scroll from her mouth; she pulled out the last of her hair and scattered it like feathers. Some of it fell into our water glasses where it floated, feathers on a river, caught in an eddy, going nowhere. We answered the door and it was her mother. There was a strange feeling inside us all the time. Inside us was a white day, but we could not go there, could not remember it. We had a sense we were standing at the end of something like a dock, something else spread out flat and fathomless before us. Our husbands honked and flapped their wings.

Her mother was a cardboard box. On her mother's side was stamped This End Up and Fragile in red block letters. On her mother's open flap someone had written her address with a black, felt-tip pen. We didn't know what we expected her to do. All the lights in the house were blue and green. Nothing had changed; the music was too loud. Right at that moment our mothers were calling our homes, trying to get a hold of us. We hadn't thought it through. She came. The man went. Her mother was on the porch. It was raining and her mother was getting wet. There was a sound like droning, a sound like wings beating against the water. "Mother Box," she said. "Mother Box," she said. "Mother Box," she said. Her mother didn't say anything. Absentmindedly, we continued eating the snacks. After all we had been through, after all we had done. "Put your hand here," we told our husbands, but they had gone out through the back door. She went to her mother and crawled inside her. She turned around three times like a dog. It was a terrible place to be, to remember. "What WEEP," she sang. We don't know when she fell asleep, or when we all did. In the morning, when the sun reached the tops of the beeches, we were surprised to discover that nothing had changed.

Conversation

The conversation they were having was about Dannie's recent pregnancy. How to plan at once for a birth and a funeral. Her friend pushed the double stroller and, at ten o'clock, the day had already become threatening.

Recently, Dannie had met a woman named Mrs. White. This in itself was not remarkable, but the woman's first name was Rose. She was an old woman, thrice-over a widow, and she worked in a shop selling jeweled hatpins in the shape of bumblebees, scallop-shell treasure chests, tiny slivers of the original cross suspended in a ruby tear and all sorts of other charms. The shop was owned by Mrs. White's friend, another Mrs. White whose first name was Lily. Dannie was very taken with this story. In it she heard something like a prophecy, though her friend's name was Sylvia and they hadn't known each other very long.

They had gone around the block several times already. Their houses sat side by side in the middle of the island. Two miles in one direction was the bay, two miles in the other the ocean, and the neighborhood went downhill very quickly. On their walks, they turned left four times: once at the red-brick Baptist church, again at the house with new copper guttering, third time at the bungalow with bed sheets for curtains and lastly at Sylvia's house, her garden newly planted with pansies, her eaves in need of paint.

They came to the corner and started again up the hill. Dannie considered her own house. Sylvia's house's twin, but freshly painted—an inner-sanctum pink, she liked to think of it, while Sylvia's house was garish, a squawking green. On Dannie's porch was her wooden swing, her red table. Also two plastic baby swings, side-by-side, so her babies could dangle their fat legs above the rhododendrons. Truly, she had been through it!

"You tell me what you would have done," she said to Sylvia. "Is it possible not to be ironic in that situation?"

But Sylvia was not fully listening. She was aware they were being watched, a man sitting on the porch of the blue Federalist house which had been sectioned into apartments, smoking a cigarette. Oh, he was harmless enough. What was his name? Steven? But it changed the way Sylvia thought of herself on this walk, changed the way she listened. She was aware of her bun, greasy and too tight. She was aware of how wide her friend's buttock had become, rolling extravagantly under her black yoga pants, and the way no one would think, though she tightened her grip on the stroller, what she was pushing around was her own. "I am a stork," thought Sylvia, but it was unclear even to herself if she was referring to her playground nickname or referencing the myth of conception her mother had insisted on during Sylvia's puberty and returned to with an almost religious fervor in the facility they had picked out together during the early years of her mother's decline.

Dannie had met the first Mrs. White through sheer chance. She had been to the bedding shop. She had just replaced her bedding and there was something complicated about the pillows, a color scheme she couldn't get right. She needed a visual aid, and then there she was, bawling in the parking lot, in her sixth month and already big as a house, as she liked to say. Dannie thought of her house, all the rooms freshly painted, the long cool hallways and the speckles of paint she still had to sand off the floorboards and would sand as soon as she could find the time. Also the underside of the windowsills to paint, the blinds to dust and straighten, a loose washer on the kitchen faucet, a strange smell wafting up the drain in the tub. A house is as bad as a baby, she liked to say. Maybe as bad as two babies, which brought her back to the point. Really, Sylvia slunk along. A front wheel of the stroller was turning blindly, rattling over the occasional divots in the sidewalk. She gave it a little kick to straighten things out.

"I mean what?" Dannie said. "Even just picking the flowers. Carnations? Baby's Breath?"

They had reached the top of the hill and paused for a moment at the foot of the church steps, directly across from the blue house. This was perhaps the highest hill on the island and they could see the bay glimmering in the distance. It seemed very flat and dark, a clouded, blind sort of blue. Sylvia knew the bay's ecological function and was familiar with its shallows rife with urchin and seagrasses, but it was hard just now to think of the bay as any kind of shelter. Its half-moon seemed a sickle rather than a horn. On the porch, the man—Robert? John?—lit another cigarette and leaned forward to grind out the first butt in the mouth of a ceramic planter shaped like a fish. He had an almost perfectly round head and his hands too seemed round, as if he could spread out his fingers and describe between the thumb and the littlest finger a geometrically perfect circle. Because of his round head, his features had an uneasy relationship with one another. From a certain angle, Sylvia had always thought him quite attractive, but then he would turn or the light would change and his jaw would be revealed as weak, his eyebrows confused, his upper lip short and petulant, soft and pursed as if he were puckering for a facetious kiss.

A wind was blowing steadily at their backs. This was the second time Dannie had kicked the stroller, jolting the whole contraption to its side wheels, and Sylvia did not know why she was now laughing. At least it wasn't a hot day, though it had seemed like it was heading that way when Sylvia got up that morning. Another ash-white day is what it looked like they were getting, but now the sky had darkened, ratcheting everything down a few degrees, and the tops of the tall pines were starting to toss back and forth. This was the kind of light that made everything look queer—patio furniture, a lawnmower, a half empty bag of potting soil—and she supposed it also made her look queer, accentuating her angles and shadows. A marabou stork, perhaps, with a mottled scalp and cruel, opportunistic beak. Dirty, clanking feathers.

Sylvia looked over to her friend, her neighbor really, but Dannie seemed consumed with her story, showing Sylvia with her hands just how big the big pillows were and how small were the small ones. Steven, she had decided to call him for convenience sake, had come down off the porch and was poking around in the shrubbery next to his driveway, a stinking tangle of sumac and poke-weed. For a moment, Sylvia felt the urge to call out to him, warn him against the poke which was poisonous and would stain his shoes if he snapped one of the thick, purple stalks. Then she imagined how she would seem to him, peering at him with her bossy eyes which, when she tried to seem kind, crinkled into pudgy imbecility. Far away behind them came a rumbling that could have been thunder or someone's truck gearing down to take a hill.

Mrs. White had been sitting in a lawn chair outside the shop smoking a cigarette. She was using a conch shell for an ashtray and her hair was piled on top of her head in an elaborate fashion that required much underpinning, struts and braces clearly visible through her thin yellow-gray curls. She had a wide mouth, pulled down slightly to the left, and she brought the cigarette to that lax side so the smoke poured out and spilled over her chin without volition or direction. It was like looking at a dragon armored entirely in pearls. Mrs. White was wearing a tee-shirt which said Palm Springs in fading pink script and featured a jungle-green palm tree accentuated at all its points with clusters of rhinestones, but this did nothing to diminish what Dannie had immediately identified as her native gravity. A practical sort of obtuseness which surrounded her as she looked past Dannie—lowing in the parking lot with her packages and the helpful chart the bedding store clerk had drawn for her and her great looming belly casting its own shadow like a miniature planet, for god's sake—and pretended to be watching the traffic pass on the causeway. At the time, this had seemed a kind of challenge to Dannie, though she conceded this was true of most situations at that stage due to hormones and worry, the worry worse even than the hormones which were, after all, natural. She had risen to it the way she rose to all challenges. Every one of them that had come her way since she was sixteen years old, just a baby really, and her life somehow seemed to slip out of gear.

"I marched right over to her," Dannie said, halting the procession to adjust the stroller's sun-shade against the slanting light. "I let her know what was going on right in front of her, but which she had refused to recognize due to her own sufferings, which were apparent, but that are nevertheless a part of being alive." Dannie loved this part of the story. She replayed it in her mind some nights while trying to fall asleep against the hum of the baby monitor, the neighbor-up-the-street's husky yodeling mournfully at the end of his chain and the palms in Sylvia's side yard clacking their hollow, gray fronds together like two immense, desiccated birds shifting their weight. Clack Clack Clack, all night. Softly, she conceded, but with great purport right outside her window as if reminding her they were still there, older than her, had been there first, rooted their whole life in exactly that soil. Another challenge! She knew the world by now; it couldn't fool her.

Dannie pictured her face as she told Mrs. White about her condition, the real life drama, the human passion of it, and she pictured it proud: her neck drawn back, cheeks highly colored, nostrils flared and quivering with the extremity of her emotion. Of course, there had been no mirror and the window of the shop was too dusty and cluttered with items for her to catch the image of herself. Mrs. White, in any event, had reacted only by blinking, her eyes delightfully out of sync so the effect was something like watching an alligator at the nature park decide whether or not it is going to submerge. She had gestured toward the lawn chair next to her. "Well, sit down," she had said, and then, "poor creature," shaking her hand toward the chair, her many bracelets jangling, her rings catching a dull light behind each of her swollen knuckles.

"You said all that?" said Sylvia, but she still could not make herself fully listen. Steven was walking down the street behind them. Out for a stroll, hands in his pockets, stopping now and then to admire the survivors of someone's late-season lilies, proud heads bobbing high above all their decapitated neighbors, or to tie over and over again his shoe. Only, he seemed to keep the distance between them exactly. Only, as they reached the house with new copper guttering and turned left, Steven also reached the house and turned left, his footsteps heavy and measured and surely a little over-loud, deliberately over-loud, behind them. Sylvia tried to focus on other things. The guttering, for example, was starting to weather, taking on an oily sheen, and she tried to remember when exactly it had been new. Was it even this year? But the image had no location, no real limits. There it was, the flash of the copper against the maroon brick, and there again were her thoughts on first seeing it: how much it must have cost/clearly, the wife didn't work, home all day, her idea/one hoped it wouldn't be stolen, copper so expensive now, people in the neighborhood just wandering through, looking for what they could get. It came back to her in that particularly synchronous way private thoughts are remembered. Her body too, how she had felt and the angle of her vision, but none of the other telling details like the shade of the sky or the quality of the light. Just herself and the copper guttering, the copper guttering, herself, herself, the guttering—

It was sickening how everything in her head repeated. Really, it was enough to make her sick, woozy as the street sloped sharply downward and she braced herself against the stroller's pull. For a moment, she imagined just letting go, the stroller rocketing crazily down the hill like a scene from some funny movie. A comedy about women, but still starring Steven who would sprint out ahead of them and save the day. They stopped so Dannie could pull the sun shade back again and behind them Steven also stopped. They started and she heard his shoe scrape against the sidewalk.

It didn't matter, it didn't matter. The house with the copper guttering was large, but the family had too many children. Sylvia had never been able to get an accurate count. The children were all around the same age, but looked very different: one with dark hair and black, almond shaped eyes, two towheads, a little girl with the raw, buff face of mental retardation. They came and went, some piling into the wife's van while others played in the backyard or sat on the front porch steps pushing clacking wooden toys. Perhaps she ran some kind of center, but the backyard as they glimpsed it through the wrought-iron fence was filled with a sort of simple clutter that seemed very private to Sylvia. Many of the border stones around the flower beds were turned side-ways and boards were nailed haphazardly to the elm tree to form crooked, unsteady looking rungs. Toys had been left to lie where they'd been dropped, beaks or truck-beds agape, and there was a dog, some tall, sleek breed which thrust its head between the bars and sniffed them with a disinterested, liver-colored nose. The dog sniffed at Steven, too. It didn't matter. It seemed no one but the dog was home.

Before them, the sky had massed into a heaving dusky purple shot through here and there with streaks of yellow. The high, burning clouds of summer had descended and streamed now over their heads, fleet and mean, weirdly bright as they whipped toward the bay. Sylvia imagined what the ocean must look like beneath that coming storm. She imagined it had risen to the oc-casion, was itself heaving, hysterical, impressionable. In the end, it was the ocean that would do the most damage to the island. A slow erosion of the land and the things that had been made of the land: the piers and shops and pavilions, the fountains and rickety crab shacks, the houses with their sandy curbsides and carefully banked garden soil. Her mother had always said the ocean was like a little brother—foolish and easily led, but once it got going, boy, look out! Her mother said the ocean had something to prove, but Sylvia was an only child and as far as she knew her mother was also an only child. They had lived alone together all of Sylvia's young life in a little house near the mouth of the bay. The island was so narrow there that in her bed at night Sylvia could hear both the impassioned tossing of the ocean's waves and the more cir-cumspect murmuring of the bay. In the season, the oyster-rakes passed back and forth over the beds just beyond her window. It had not been idyllic. There was no air-conditioning and the sump-pump yielded up a steady trickle of gritty, brackish water from around the foundation, but to Sylvia it had been very real and so constant she remembered every surface and angle of the house in a still, clear, inviolate light as if it had never been visited by her own experiences. As if it were a place wholly independent of her, enduring, to which the fact of herself was incidental and easily overlooked.

The house was no longer there. The whole area had been leveled to make way for a Palmetto Bank and a parking lot, a Build-Your-Own Burrito restaurant with a flashy lanai complete with taxidermied parrots and cane-benches cemented into the ground. In fact, the only marker of her childhood that still stood was a corrugated-steel warehouse which had housed in its time an auto-body shop, construction materials and then sand dredged from the deep ocean rifts to replenish the beaches after storms. The occasional fiddler crab would stray from the bay's mudflats and set up a territory in those artificial dunes, loiter in the cracked hanger doors with its swollen, belligerent claw drawn up before its eyes. Now the warehouse was a church called the First Holiness Spiritual Center in Christ, but it endured regardless. As did the bay, of course. And the ocean.

Steven stumbled over something. Sylvia heard him swear under his breath, closer than she had thought. "Let's cut through the alley," Dannie said. "It looks like it's going to rain."

After her encounter with the first Mrs. White, Dannie had gone back to the store frequently. The season was changing, but in such a begrudging fashion she found it difficult to mark the time, and already her body was no use to her. She was so large her size seemed a condition of her being. Like a blimp, she thought, but not in any old way. Not in the way the pregnancy guide books had encouraged her to figure—full like a fruit, or a pod from which would be squeezed perfectly identical peas—but rather full like a hovering disaster filled with swirling miasmic gasses, waiting for the spark. She explained herself in this way to Mrs. White who nodded and produced a string of tiny, bone beads, each carved into a rudimentary face, dug-out hollows for the eyes, slashed mouths partially open.

"Lover's chain,' said Mrs. White and pooled the little heads in Dannie's hand.

"I know what you mean," Dannie said. "I have never been one to shy away from the truth."

Oh, it had been, she now realized, some kind of salad days. All around the island, the jessamine had been blooming and falling off, blooming again. Her feet were distant, mysterious conveyances. She heard them as she went, rustling through the dropped bells, shushing in the brittle drifts discarded by the plant's swelling seeds. She and the Mrs. Whites sat in the front window beneath the air conditioning vent and watched cars sweep back and forth on the causeway like water bugs. Occasionally a truck would pass and they could see the bridge dip and sway below its weight, bob for long minutes afterward in a kind of gracile indecision.

"How many, do you think, if the bridge collapsed?" Dannie would ask. "How many if it happened right now?"

And the Mrs. Whites would laugh, one following the other, descending notes spilling creakily out to the corners of the crowded room.

She and the Mrs. Whites sifted through the store's objects. An inventory of unusual shells, carved do-dads, glass balls into which were blown smaller glass balls and inside those: bubbles, pin-points of emptiness which caught the light. Everything was covered with a thin layer of dust, yellowed as if cellophane had been slid over her eyes. She and the Mrs. Whites picked out fabrics from the store's back room. Sateen, pink polka-dotted organdy, a slick of water-shot silk that could be pinned and twisted into bunting, a romantic little spill of lace. It was going to be a party. She and the Mrs. Whites planned to drink mint lemonade and eat finger foods. Red sausages wrapped in pastry dough, a blonde pudding studded with figs. They would wear dresses, little ankle socks. She imagined the Mrs. Whites fooling around in the sandy loam in their ankle socks, a stiff frill of lace cupping their ankle bones, tasteful plastic plates of cake they could gesture with, should they so choose, toward the dais or the horizon, the little box cozened in flowers and fabrics, the bridge flanked by its attendant gulls dipping and bowing in the evening light. Perhaps there would be an exigency planned for nightfall. Tiki-torches, a fire pit. Why not braziers placed at thoughtful intervals along the path back to the parking lot? Dannie loved the idea of shadows lapping against the stones all the way down the crooked hill. Like the sound of the bay lapping. Little waters, nothing really. An eddy, a shallow. The storm already passed safely out to sea.

And then she had the babies.

Then she had both of her babies.

Both of her babies had then been born.

Sylvia did not understand why they were still talking about this. It had been months and the babies were fine. A boy and a girl, both sleeping in the stroller and healthy seeming if small, their sharp faces screwed up against the fitful light. There had been something wrong with the boy's legs. They had curved in a strange way, the feet coming together below his torso like another set of hands, the way she imagined a baby monkey's feet would bend to clasp. Sylvia had found this charming and the baby boy did not seem bothered by it. In their earliest days, Dannie had invited Sylvia to the house to marvel over the babies, both stretching fretfully in one crib, and the boy had kicked off his blankets and clapped his strange feet together. The look on his face made Sylvia feel he was threatening her somehow, giving her a glimpse of his proud, severe future, but he was an infant—only a few weeks old—and she knew his face bore no indication of his emotions. Still, Sylvia liked the baby boy. Even now that his legs were encased in braces, the soft bones being bent straight, she preferred him to his sister who was plump and creamy, her joints banded with rosy folds of skin. The girl yawned prettily in the stroller, her mouth as neat as a cat's, and when she pressed her lips back together and tucked her soft chin against her neck, Sylvia thought she could see some shade of the girl's adulthood cross her face, some shadow even of her old womanhood. The crepe neck wrinkling into her collar, the sweetheart chin soft as a dumpling. She would always look this way, Sylvia thought, pretty and vulnerable, soft and tempting.

Sometimes Dannie would call Sylvia over and have her hold one or the other of the babies to keep them occupied while she attended some task of the house. "Just bounce her a little," Dannie would say. "She likes it when you blow on her head." But Sylvia was discomfited by the girl child. She found herself constantly fighting the urge to pinch her on the inside of her elbows or the backs of her knees, to take the tiny fold of her ear between her lips and, very gently, bite. It was different with the boy. She respected him. She supposed she felt deferential to him and to what she inferred were his clear preferences. Peas, for example, over pears. The flash of the keys on Dannie's keychain over the sandy cush-cush of the white-noise machine. Both of the babies' eyes had darkened, but the girl's had become a sort of mossy green while the boy's had complicated—a blue shot through with indigo, a gray striated by navy. Like clouds, Sylvia thought, like these clouds lowering now over their heads as they turned down the alley. Like the lid of a bucket levering shut.

Sylvia thought too much, that was for certain. Her mother had always said this about her with something in her voice both of pride and approbation. In church, her mother said this about her to the other mothers as they gathered around the folding metal table spread with platters of pastel cookies and Styrofoam coffee cups, the rims smeared with equally pastel lip-prints: shimmering pink, oyster cream, chill lavender. Sylvia's own mother had never worn lipstick, and where were the other children? Sylvia scoured her memory for them, but found only her mother in a green serge skirt, her hands thrust into the skirt's deep pockets, rocking back on her kitten heels. A thinker, her mother had described her to the other mothers, but Sylvia had always thought of herself more as a witness. She saw the colors, heard the whispers, felt the damp heat of the breeze. She remembered the nap of the carpet in the church basement, a hard industrial nub, and the coarse, split feel of her mother's knuckles as she reached into her mother's pocket to take her hand. There was so much all around her. So much always going on between the bay and the ocean, the weather, the demands of the seasons one after another, and now her neighbor, Dannie, whose motion lights were too sensitive and struck on at the slightest breeze to shine in her bedroom window, who left the television on for company in her dark house so its blue light gathered and pattered and flashed into the dawn, who thrust her torso over the porch railing and called to her—"Sylvie! Sylvie! Are you there?"—to come over, come over, for a minute come over, come with her on another walk around the block.

When would there ever be time to think about any of this? It seemed to Sylvia as if she had been gathering herself for the effort. As if, for a long time, the materials she would need had been washing into her like flotsam caught in an eddy, and soon she would array them all before her, the stuff of her life, and really *think* about it the way her mother had always assumed she would.

What would her life have been? Ladyfinger cookies and paper plates, a lace embroidered handkerchief, an aquamarine hairnet and jet beads hanging in an unraveling fringe from the flap of a handbag.

What would it have been? A loose screen flapping against the window, the pop of ice fracturing in a glass, the rustle of underskirts, nylon thighs, the clack of short heels measuring up and down a hall.

What else could it have been? The taste of cream fillings, of powdered cheeses, the bite of grass sucked at its sweet root. The raw iron oyster of blood. The brine of the ocean. The thick massy rot of the bay.

The baby boy made a sound almost like a bark and when Sylvia peered over the sun-shade to check on him, she found he had twisted against the strap that held him in place, craned his neck to look up at her. The metal joints of his braces glinted an oily light at his knees and ankles. His bare feet flexed at the end of this armature and looked slightly swollen, tinged purple as if Dannie had cinched the straps too tight across his thighs. It was a shame his legs had lost the ability to gesture, though in the end, she conceded, the braces would make them more useful for walking. And that was what they were for, after all, Sylvia told herself. Was that not what a child's legs were for? At the far end of the alley two cherry trees tossed their limbs back and forth, streaming together in the wind so it seemed the alley did not empty again into the road, but into a wild green cacophony, a frenzy. Behind her, very close, Sylvia heard Steven clear his throat and thought, looking down into the baby boy's fierce eyes, Now Now Now Now Now.

But even as she thought it, she recognized the question. The wind flattened against them in a huge, coughing pant and it seemed to Sylvia as if their shadows danced around them. Her shadow and Dannie's shadow, the babies' hydra shadow craning out of their stroller and Steven's cast before him, so close now it pressed into their own. It was as if the light of the day were a bulb swinging loose from the sky, knocking around crazily, shining onto all sides of them at once. "Now?" thought Sylvia. "Is it now? now? now?"

And now *this*, is what Dannie was thinking. She was busy, of course, the way everyone had said she would be busy. There was the house to keep up, the babies to bed down. An incredible disorder had taken hold of her refrigerator where, in the bottom of the crisper, something had liquefied into a foul sepia slurry. It also held sway in her linen closet where the towels were neither folded, nor rolled, but smashed into wrinkled wads, the hand towels and bath towels tangling together, the babies' soft swaddling blankets twisting like pastel snakes in and out of the shelves. Soon she would have to go back to work, her leave almost spent, and that would add another layer to her day. The traveling layer. The hurrying layer. Her breasts were hugely swollen, the veins so prominent along their bulging sides it was as if her skin had thinned to isinglass. The smallest thing set them off. A cat yowling in the yard, a particular series of notes played on a record, the call of the garbage men high over the rumbling of their truck as they scoured the blue morning streets, and her breasts ached and leaked. In fact, everything about her leaked. Breast milk darkened the front of her shirts, drool slipped from the side of her mouth as she dropped into an exhausted afternoon nap, blood and other mucous flux slid in streamers from the still lax muscles of her vagina.

It was no different from incontinence, Dannie thought. She was no different from some species of giant, incontinent snail hauling her outlandish, gaudy shell about the house as she picked up a baby, washed a pan, put down a baby, proffered a breast, sipped weak coffee out of a dirty mug, and slicked her airy house with her effluvium. The wet of her trailed in clotted swathes across her floors and furniture, walls and window-glass. Anyone could see it. It was filthy, foul. She was supposed to be emptied now, the loose skin of her stomach doubling the elastic of her waistband as a reminder, but here she was still filled with the waste-material. Mucous, useless veins, milk and blood.

One of the babies hiccupped with the preoccupied breathiness that was the precursor to a wail and Dannie reached across Sylvia to joggle the stroller. Movement was supposed to be soothing. Well, they were moving. It seemed to Dannie as if all she did just now was move. Around the block over and over again. Turn left and left and left and left, always with Sylvia, always in this strange season—a blooming, bruised, sullen summer that had come to the island months and months ago and seemed in no hurry to leave. And now it was going to rain again. And now something was wrong with Sylvia, always something wrong with Sylvia, who stared ahead of them down the alley with a fixed, strained expression such as someone might wear if they caught sight of a meteorite, impossibly far but getting closer, bearing down over their head.

Dannie looked from Sylvia's face, down the length of the alley and back again. It all looked the same as usual: The chain link fences smothered with honey-suckle and poison ivy. The skeleton of a neighbor's greenhouse project, unglassed, but stuffed anyway with stands of tomato, small furred ferns, pots of herbs left to bloom and seed. Dannie had not been back to see the Mrs. Whites since the babies were born. It seemed a rude disappointment, these two healthy babies in their white cotton onesies, the event they had so looked forward to definitively cancelled, and she felt the least she could do for the old ladies was delay. After all, let's be practical. How long could they have? The Mrs. Whites so bent they were like swamp roots, wavering from the earth only to turn and dive once again. The Mrs. Whites in their dark, dirty store, barely mobile, cleaved in turn by ocean light as it scythed through their window on the way to the bay. And come to think of it, where was that store exactly? Pregnant, Dannie had navigated as if by tides, a swelling drift pushing her toward the causeway, pulling her back to the little neighborhood, the little house, the little neighbor shut up like a bug behind her little, green front door. Now, Dannie felt a dangerous, unfamiliar volition. It was as if her self, her real self called Dannie, was a skinny, electrified nerve encased in pulpy layers of fat and blood. As if, should the nerve get out of the house, put on pants that buttoned, pack the babies into the complicated struts of their car seats and steer them all out onto a main street, where it went from there could not be predicted. What rules did a nerve have? Did it have any rules, any behavioral stricture other than to feel, to thrum, to buzz? Where would a nerve go if it had all the world in which to foray? How could it ever bring itself to stop?

One of the babies made a husky, throttled noise. It was not of their usual repertoire. Not a sound that portended or precluded, and though Dannie did not feel alarmed—she had never been, would never be, a woman bitten along the edges with useless care—she did feel some interior part of her quicken and turn. Her damn breasts again, but no, they were dry, she herself dry, and the wind buffeting her limbs like thick cotton. Dannie leaned over the stroller and looked down at her children. The boy was twisted around in his seat, his forehead wide and smooth, his eyes blue and troubling. They were hers, it occurred to her. He and his sister, every moment of them under her ownership, at least for now. It was a cheering thought. Maybe she would take them to see the Mrs. Whites after all, painting their faces first as if she and the babies had all just swept in from some outdoor event replete with balloons and colorful exhibitions of skill. Just because the crux of the conversation had changed didn't mean it couldn't continue, couldn't evolve to include the unimagined perils inherent in being the mother of two healthy children. And wasn't it the unknown that was supposed to be so enticing? Wasn't that, after all, what the Mrs. Whites had designed their store to sell?

Dannie imagined depositing each baby in the crooked cradle of a Mrs. Whites lap—the girl painted up like a beaver, little buck teeth lapping onto her sharp chin, and the boy something else, something the Mrs. Whites would approve of. An insect perhaps, garishly alien, his legs already so many jointed it was no great feat to imagine them twisted back above his head, rubbing out a measuring tune. She imagined the expressions on the old ladies' alligator faces, their mouths widening like cracks crazing through varnish, their ropy knuckles popping as they bent their hands to grasp. Delightful! These anthropomorphic babes, these little mummers. Curios, apologies, proffered gifts.

This is what Dannie was thinking when she recognized the sound behind her as running footsteps only a second before the blow landed at the base of her skull. A great blackness bloomed and the world pressed around her, a last lashing fever, as she fell.

Sylvia's mother had believed in many unfashionable ideas. Fortitude and mutability, tenacity and penance. In her last years, her suspicion of the world grew deeper and she saw everywhere around her evidence of an endemic failure to transform. Evidence that evolution had reached its standstill. "There's nothing left to look forward to," she told Sylvia, tracing one finger along the back of her daughter's hand. Out her mother's window Sylvia could see a little manicured square of the facility's lawn, then the cracked expanse of parking lot, then a row of tourist cottages, identical rainbow wind-socks fluttering at each front door. It was a late summer day, high season. If the window could open Sylvia might have opened it to hear the shattered cheer of the beach, each voice heaving itself momentarily up out of the mass of voices, clear and bright, gilded with sun. She might have sat with her mother and had another sort of conversation entirely, touched there in her mother's white room by the unknown lives that had always accompanied them, partners in the shared square of warmth and salt and faint, fading spray. But the building was an institution, the window built as an idea of a wall and the air fluorescent with artificial chill as the air conditioner kicked up another notch. "No more freaks," her mother said, resting her hand on the back of her daughter's hand for the last time in either of their lives. "No more monsters."

Yet, here is her daughter, many years later, turning to face what surely comes next. Around her roars the surf from which all such monsters have crawled. They rattle their saber limbs, cast pale snouts to test an unfamiliar wind.

The Dinner Party

She has prepared the dinner, but the guests are late. The foods sit in their various serving bowls, wrapped snugly in foil. In rotation, she tents each foil top just slightly to let out steam and condensation. The kitchen fills with intermingled smells.

On the third rotation, the guests arrive. It feels to her as if she has been standing in the kitchen for days—chopping and slicing, deboning and trimming the scales, basting, brazing, deglazing pans, beating together eggs and sugar, eggs and sugar, eggs and sugar until stiff peaks hang like mock icicles from the end of her whisk.

"I'm so sorry we're late," says Diane. Her husband stands in the doorway behind her holding a serving platter draped in a dinner-party themed kitchen towel. The towel is patterned with martini glasses and open mouths laughing. There is a woman's mouth and a man's mouth. The woman-mouths are misprinted so their lipstick hangs just below their lip-lines like carnelian ghosts and the man-mouths are crowned with trim black moustaches which remind her viscerally of Diane's husband, though he is clean shaven and smiles at her, nods toward the bottle of wine he has clamped in the crook of his arm.

She reminds herself she is often reminded only of what is directly in front of her, that this is a failing of hers, and they all tumble into the kitchen to eat toast points crowned with various savory spreads, drink cocktails and watch as she puts the finishing touches on a dish she has set aside, unfinished, for just this purpose.

"I've always believed the chive was an immature onion," says Diane. She laughs. "Can you believe until this very moment that's what I've always thought?"

It is her husband, the host, who has set Diane straight on this matter. He has just now emerged from the back of the house, where it seems to her he has loitered almost exclusively for the past many months, and stands blinking against the low light of the kitchen. He is wearing his work clothes, the shirt ripped at the shoulder seam so she can see a pale diamond of his skin, and has tucked his spectacles into his shirt pocket.

"That's alright," her husband says, clearing his throat first, a little hoarse, "that's your prerogative."

Everyone laughs in a sincere way. They are good friends; it is alright to admire each other. Diane whose hip curves like a cold moon at the top of her jeans. Diane's husband who seats himself at the table, his plate bare before him, and smiles at her as she adds the chives, at last, to the dish.

Then, the eating begins. There are many dishes and they pass them around and around. The plates are soon slick with juices and beside them her husband and Diane's husband build growing cairns of bones. Diane picks up two bones from her husband, the host's, plate and slips them into the sides of her mouth so they bob like whiskers. The bones are translucent, sliver thin. This is an old joke among them. They are celebrating something—Diane is pregnant again or they have bought a larger house—and Diane's husband toasts to the celebration, to the meal. He rinses his mouth with wine and moves his chair closer to her, the hostess, so when he turns to smile at her she can feel the heat coming off his dark face, waves of heat, and sees, she believes, that his dark eyes are blacker than she had ever thought them to be. They shine in his face like polished beads and when he blinks she believes she can still see them shining.

"Another toast!" says her husband, the host, and when he reaches across the table to clink his glass the tear in his shirt gaps and yaws like a tiny, diamond-shaped mouth. There is a smell from him. A russet smell like the one in the back of their house, which reminds her of rust, something has rusted, the pipes?, something below the house crumbling so what is contained within it pours out. It is a problem they were supposed to have dealt with a long time ago. "To us!" her husband says, draining the wine from his glass.

It has gotten louder in the room. Someone has turned the music on, turned it up. Diane's husband passes his wife another chop, a little pot of mustard and the mustard paddle with which to slather. She herself is full, she is sure of it, but fills her plate again—root and seed, muscle, flower.

"It's all so delicious," Diane says. "Incomparable!"

Diane is very white and taut, she realizes. Even whiter and more smoothly muscled than she had remembered from their many many, uncountable many, dinner parties of the past. She seems to glow, in fact, incomparably, and is hard to look at as she holds her naked fork in the air, dips it as if conducting the music. Her husband, the host, emits a sudden squeal and scrabbles at the table. He has dropped his spoon into the soup, cannot find it.

His eyes have grown very small or his face very large. His eyes are almost totally enfolded by his face and he cannot see. His roving hands are clumsy, spill wine and gravy, and Diane's husband dips his sleek head to his plate in seeming sympathy. He turns to face her so she alone can see he is laughing, his black eyes wet with it, and he unfurls his quick tongue so it just grazes her wrist, long and light and dry.

The music is too loud! She cannot hear what anyone is saying. But there is still dessert to be had—the masterpiece—and still in the center of the table Diane's dish covered with its towel which, now that she notices, has darkened at the center as if sopping something, wicking it away.

"What is this music?" she asks. "If it's *Scheherazade* that was my grandmother's favorite," but even as she says it she is rising, moving into the kitchen. The dessert has been chilling in the refrigerator and when she sees it again she is relieved to find it still pristine, unaged. It stands alone on the center shelf, the cool of the fridge a blue shadow below its peaks. She feels a great love for this dessert, almost a swooning for it. She lifts it as she might an animal, a docile one, though one whose habits remain uncertain. The music swells and peters. It is *Scheherazade*, she is sure, and she turns to the table, the dessert held before her, smiling so that her teeth will show, but what of it? They are friends. It is a party.

And yet, what is this? She sees Diane has uncovered her dish. The men are cheering, her husband tilting his head back, holding a fold of flesh up and away from his eye with one blunt hand. Diane's husband has laid his head fully on the table as if to get a better view of her dish, which is, she will admit, incomparable—dark, rich, heaving slightly in the very bright light that pours from Diane's hands, spills from the deep cleft of her neckline.

"Oh, no darling," says Diane, motioning her forward. "Yours is too beautiful. You mustn't mind. You don't mind? Put it here, right on the table. Let's look at them together. Cheers."

But it is really too late. She knows that. She can picture how her dessert will look on the table, littered now with dishes, stained, the tablecloth askew and in some places tattered. She has failed her dessert, failed its dear crevices, its frail, tremulous desires. She has failed the party, she sees, as she notices a cobweb hung thick and cloistered between the spires of the chandelier, a rung hanging down from the back of Diane's husband's chair and the borders of the rug unraveling, each thread faded to the same murky brown. There is nothing for it. She holds the dessert out in front of her.

"It had no chance, poor thing," she thinks, stepping forward. Diane's dish has somehow slipped to the side of the plate and now hangs there, pattering a warm liquid onto the table cloth. It seems to elongate as she watches, as if seeking purchase, and then there is a terrible clamor of drums, trumpets, fifes. Something insurmountable has happened to the music, and the light grows so bright, so piercing, that all she can see are Diane's husband's eyes, black, unblinking, tilted toward her as if sharing a joke.

A White Hat on His Head,
Two Wooden Legs

There was a girl who was wild and a boy who was tame. This is not to say anything, but merely how they were raised: both with great care, almost precision, but one with a stick brought down on his head every night and one who had been given a fat little book with onion-skin pages and anatomical drawings in full color therein.

One day, when they had both grown out of their plump infancy and exchanged the fine fur that swathed their limbs and torsos for coarser, more menacing stuff, their mothers packed them each a brown sack filled with bread and cheese, dried fruits and skins of milk and water and waved to them from the gates of the tidy houses in which they had previously spent all of their lives. The girl and the boy walked many miles down the roads that led from their homes which were ringed on all sides by an impenetrable forest. They were alone, but they had been raised to anticipate being alone. They were hungry, but they had been raised to expect that feeling could and should be appeased. In separate clearings, they both sat down to enjoy the first meal that had not been served to them on a thin china plate and drink the first drink they did not sip out of a chipped china cup emblazoned with their very own names.

When their appetites were satisfied both the girl and the boy took a moment to be still in their surroundings and listen to the noises the world was making. The girl ran her fingers over a tussock of moss that was growing up next to her thigh. She pinched the heads of some purple gerardia so she could better see down the length of the flowers' speckled throats. The boy closed his eyes and leaned back on his elbows. He listened to the call of a phoebe who, protecting its nest, fluttered at the forest edge canting a lame wing over its eyes. "Phoebe phoebe phoebe phoebe," the bird said and the boy pulled his stick out of his sack and ran his hands over its familiar knots. Many miles away, the girl squinted as a cloud passed over the face of the sun. She ruffled the edges of her onion-skin book so the flayed muscles within blurred together and seemed to stretch and bunch.

They traveled this way for many days. One day, the girl sat down on a log beneath a rustling oak and ate the last crumb of her bread, swallowed the last hot slug of water from her skins. The water was musty and animal. For the first time in her life, the girl was unsatisfied. She tucked her head between her knees and pressed her knees against her ears until everything sounded like the color apricot. She called out, "Oh oh oh oh," and that too sounded apricot which was a color that made her feel nauseous and even more unhappy. Soon she was inconsolable. She gnashed her teeth.

Meanwhile, the boy had taken many turns at random and found himself off the road entirely. He did not feel lost because he had not from the first day known where he was going, but he did feel uneasy. He had eaten his last morsel of cheese many hours before and had hoarded his milk so long it had gone sour in the skin. The day before, the boy had come across a swift cold stream that frothed and tinkled, but he did not drink from it because he remembered stories of both enchantment and disease. Many days before that, he had come across a bush heavy with plump red berries, but he did not eat from it because he remembered stories of pain and an enduring thirst that thickened in the mouth until the tongue went dead and grey. The boy recognized he was in dire straits, but he did not know what to do next. He supposed he would keep traveling, and then he heard a horrible noise. "Oh oh oh oh," went the noise and the boy crept forward, parting the undergrowth before him with his stick.

Of course the two met. This had been assumed from their earliest days and they were told in their childhood beds that there was another in the world who had been kept for them, groomed for them. This other person would do for them all the things their mothers had done and perform other actions as well, though what these were was a secret their mothers did not explain. So. Though in fact the boy and the girl met as strangers and were alone in the forest, a dangerous place, and one of them was howling and one of them was carrying before him a fiercely knotted stick, neither the boy nor the girl felt alarm or threat. Rather, they greeted each other with calm recognition. As if to say, "Good to see you again," in the sort of situation where this is expected, but not fully believed.

That evening, the boy and the girl slept at the base of the great oak. Through the overlapping branches, they could sometimes see stars.

"Did you come a long way?" asked the boy who had put his arm under the girl's head so she could use it as a pillow.

"Far enough," said the girl, pinching the skin along the boy's ribs with the tips of her very sharp nails. She had right away apprehended the uses of the stick and left behind her a trail of inflamed wheals which made the boy sigh happily and soon put him to sleep.

Indeed, the children, for they were still that, turned out to be most symbiotic. The girl showed the boy the pictures in her book which he found altogether too red, too linear. Though he did not share it, he recognized her fascination and in response the boy took off his clothes and let her touch and bend, stretch and manipulate all the parts she had previously understood without dimension but which now confronted her whole and unexamined, functioning without the knowledge of their innermost chambers. Which she had. Which she treasured.

When the boy rose in response to her touch, he showed her how to make a ring between her thumb and index finger, where to stroke, how hard to squeeze. The first time, he guided her hand with his own atop it and when he came and his semen washed over her wrist he called her attention to the change in his spent texture, to the vein that pulsed thickly along the side of his withering sac. Having understood them only through pictures, she had never known how quickly a body could alter its forms. As she was wild, her own body had never been a conveyance for her. She *was* her body and so incapable of figuring her self as a separate, interior passenger, incapable of imagining an alternative to what she had just done or what it was she might do next. She felt a weeping tide of gratitude that this boy and his body had come into her life.

In thankfulness, the girl picked up the boy's stick and beat him about the head and torso. She cracked bloody knots in his shoulders, split open his eyebrow, burst his mouth like a plum. It had been so many days since the boy had been beaten that he too felt weak with gratitude. As he lay shaking on the forest floor, he looked up at the girl framed by the tree's tossing limbs and shards of sky winking blue as mirrors. He said, "I love you," and she said, "Don't talk." In this fashion, they knew each other.

As the days passed and they traveled through the forest, the girl and the boy experimented with roots and berries. They drank from the cups of mushrooms so white they glimmered in the forest darkness and chewed strips of bark they pulled from trees which first filled their mouth with an oily fire before softening to a green tingle that numbed them from within. It was clear they could not live in this provisional fashion for long. Already, they had become very thin and what muscles were left hung slack from their bones. Already, they felt a pervasive exhaustion and the girl's lustrous eyes seemed smaller and harder and the boy's rich brown hair hung lank and dull.

Then one day, quite suddenly, they passed out of the forest and into the skirting fields of a small town. As it turned out, this was just in time. The boy collapsed onto the warm, turned soil and the girl dug into the ground, using her hands like paws. She turned up two wizened potatoes and held them in front of her, considering, while the sun, always before so dappled and fleeting, beat down on her head with a feeling like trumpets and clashing shields. They were out of their element, that was for sure. As far as the girl could see in one direction the field stretched in grizzled hummocks. In the other direction the girl could see buildings, their squares and tri-angles harsh and garishly overlapping after so long among only the shapes of the forest. A fan of smoke was feathering in the breeze. As she watched, another rose to join it, black at the base as if some-one were burning leaves. The girl remembered her mother saying, long ago now, in the little kitchen where almost all the meals of her life had been prepared and consumed, "Everything you need, the forest will give to you. This is a warning. I'll only say it once."

But they had been traveling so long now…But surely another sort of life had already begun…

The girl held the potatoes up to her face and inhaled their thin, yellow scent. She rubbed them over her cheeks and chin, over her lips, as if they were stones, appreciating their texture, their weight. She was just thinking, she thought. She was just pausing for breath. The girl was honestly surprised when she found, passing the potato back over her lips, that she had taken a bite but then, the morsel in her mouth both watery and sharp, her saliva flooding her teeth and her tongue, she ate the whole thing and two bites of the second. With a great effort of will, she woke the boy up and shared what was left and they sat together in silence, not yet satisfied, surrounded by a pale infinitude of shifting air in which nothing rustled and nothing snapped, from which nothing treasured them as prey or marked them a danger and skirted their location on careful feet. Eventually, they both fell asleep and slept until the sun sank to the tops of the trees and the wind of another season blew cool across the field.

Had anyone come across them, they would have seemed a picture out of some pretty book. The girl with her tattered skirt, the boy with his ragged stockings. The girl with her hollow cheeks, the boy whose face was stained and swollen. They were two children at the end of a hard time and on the next page, as such stories go, one might expect to see them further imperiled or graced by their earlier virtue with rescue in the form of a fox or an owl, the king of the field mice or a great, black swan. The truth was nothing so kind and nothing so simple. But, as they were young and alone, unobserved in a field which was shorn for the winter, they were gifted long confusing years between action and consequence. When the truth finally came it passed unremarked. As brief as a ray of light fingering through the forest. As strange as a bell tolling in the tower.

And yet, here at last, the boy and the girl had found a place where they could settle instead of a place through which they must toil. The town was large enough that no one paid attention to two new inhabitants, which was as the boy wanted. But, the town was also small enough that at least twice a month the town's people threw festivals to celebrate a detail of the year and the pageant and costume, the ritual and parade, satisfied many needs the girl had not known she possessed. The boy and the girl moved into a cottage located between the butcher's shop and the apothecary's larder. The boy built a little fence, for privacy, which he painted white and latched by means of a silver latch tied up with a thin, blue string. The girl beat the dirt floors and oiled them until the floors shone underfoot and could be swept clean of crumbs with a pine-straw broom. They had a cottage garden in which the boy planted radish and hot peppers. They kept a hutch full of rabbits which the girl fed on radish-tops and stroked between their wide, wet eyes until they went into a trance. When it came time to slit their throats, the girl did this too and she caught their blood in a silver pail and she turned them out of their skins and set their skins on the fence-posts to dry.

The boy and the girl took care of each other's needs. For a little extra money, the boy hired himself out as a butcher's apprentice. When his master was out, he would bring the girl over and show her the cuts: the shoulder which would become a goulash, the leg destined for stroganoff, the aitchbone which would be stewed and boiled, served with cabbage or made into a fine, clear soup. The girl took in the neighbors' laundry and scalded and scrubbed it, delivered it back to them tightly folded and tied with twine. In the winter months, she taught a class made up of farmers' sons and daughters who came into her tidy kitchen to learn what she could teach them of simple sums and how to sign their names, what she thought lay beyond the forest that ringed the town and what she was pretty sure did not.

In the evenings, when the boy came home, he would eat the

supper the girl had made and they would talk together about the day that had passed and the one that was coming. Then, they would retire into the bedroom where the girl had stitched thick curtains out of the remnants of their traveling clothes and the boy would show the girl new things about their bodies. After a certain time, one would think there could no longer be anything new to show, but the girl was observant, ravenous for detail, and the boy was imaginative, strong, generous with his time. When they were finished, the boy, still out of breath, would kneel in the middle of the room. The girl would take up his old knotted stick from its place by the hearth and beat him severely, the sound of her blows sometimes carrying all the way to the street where people passing by might imagine someone was chopping wood, or slapping a wet blanket against the side of the washtub so it might dry.

And so, time passed.

This happened at once very fast and with infinite tedium. On some days, the girl would amuse herself by trying to remember what it had felt like to be inside her body on the same date the year before and on the same date the year before that. Other days, when they finally lay down together to sleep, the boy would re-mark that the only clear impression he had of the day just passed was waking up that morning in the same small bed and opening his eyes. Of course, there were other, more durable markers. The girl noted that the boy had grown a single white eyelash which stood out starkly amongst his other hairs. The boy noticed that the girl had developed a fondness for cream-based sauces and on most days her lips were very chapped and rough. They neither of them remarked these things to the other, but both of them felt a spreading sort of feeling, as if they were growing to accom-modate the space allotted to them. As if they would eventually grow to press against one wall with their knees and the other with their elbows, to cant their necks against the peak of the ceiling, to shove one shoe in the black mouth of the hearth. So far would they grow, but no farther. This was a natural way to feel they both of them supposed.

One February, when the fields were grey and beaten flat by freezing rains and the forest around the town radiated darkness and rustling, the girl was teaching a class of farm and village children to sing a song.

"What kind of bird is that?" the girl sang.

And the children sang in reply, "A little bird, a black bird, a bird that flies away."

"And how does that bird eat?" sang the girl.

"A white hat on his head," the children sang. "Two wooden legs. He goes hungry."

"And how will that bird taste?" sang the girl.

And the children sang in reply, "We eat him up, we eat him up, so fast we do not know."

At this point in the song, all the children were supposed to sing sounds instead of words. The girl children were supposed to sing high and eerie sounds like icicles snapping in the silent forest and the boy children were supposed to sing low and empty sounds like the black water of a winter pond, or a winter stomach. This is what they did and as they did the girl looked out over them. The children were of all ages. Some were very young and their cheeks were bright and red with heat from her stove and excitement about the bird who had been caught and so got what he deserved. Some were quite a bit older and of these one girl and one boy in particular seemed older still.

That girl struck her as very silly. She had grown her hair longer and longer as her body grew up out of her childhood and now her hair slipped down to the wide mound her buttocks made in her skirt and fanned there stiff and coarse and unhealthy. She had plump feet which she fidgeted constantly so they rustled beneath her hem like two pale animals, and sometimes when she answered a question, the girl could see her thoughts lift and scatter like a flock of birds rising all at once from a tree.

The boy was larger than both the girl who was a student and the girl who was a teacher. His father raised red deer which he slaughtered for Christmas feasts and the boy had grown among the deer and taken up some of their aspects. He had a broad brow and round, black eyes. He sometimes craned his neck forward, as if to clear an obstruction in his throat, and when he wrote he held the pen pressed between his thick rough fingers as if it were wedged in the cleft of an overgrown hoof. As he made his low empty noises, he looked out the window spangled with frost, but the girl could tell he was neither observing the patterns nor looking beyond them to the busy street.

"Oh ho Oh ho," sang the boy who was her student. The girl found herself incapable of imagining either him or the girl as they were when they were alone. What face might they make when there was no one to see their faces? What future passions might they feel that did not involve the care and comfort of their bodies? Both of them inhabited the lunging sort of bodies possessed by people who have never been denied their fill of meat and both of them, as they made their noises, were aware of the other, of the shape made by the space where they were not. All this the girl could tell.

Yet, though she knew outside of her kitchen that boy and that girl came together in the field, in the loft, under the sacks of bloody jute stacked freezing next to the butcher's side door, she could imagine neither the pleasure they found in each other nor the pain. The girl was as blank to her as a bar of soap. The boy as empty as a pot in which the stew has been allowed to dry and stick. She had never thought about her students this way, never imagined them outside the confines of her own house. It had been as if they sprung into existence when they opened the door and faded out of it when the door latched behind them, but now that she had begun, she found she could not stop. Every face presented to her its blank possessions: two lips, two eyes, a nose, two shifting brows. But she found what she saw instead was a wavering tumult of objects. Here a child's face was obscured by a bridle; there a child's hands drifted in and out of the belly of a steaming teapot. That girl shuffled her feet and her lips seemed to blur into sheets of stiff cotton. That boy propped his chin in his hand and his shoulders squared into the blocky beam of a yoke. Slowly, as the children sang, the girl came to a terrible realization.

That evening, the girl sat at the window and watched as the boy left by the side door of the butcher's shop and locked it behind him. He waited at the corner for some carriages to pass and crossed the street in a quick trot, leaping over puddles with exaggerated spring. She lost sight of him for a moment as he rounded the fence and came in through the gate, but when he opened the door to the cottage and stood before her, she saw he was just as she had expected: breathless from cold, blood on his smock, his hair standing up from his head in a crest that made him look both impatient and like a child.

When the boy asked the girl about her day, she told him nothing about what she had thought and answered instead with all the usual details. When the girl asked the boy in turn what he had done at work, he smiled at her and chewed at her and waggled his fingers as he mocked the customers who provided them both with bread and meat.

"But what does he think?" thought the girl.

"Fat as a toad," the boy laughed. "She is round as a hat."

"But how will he taste?" the girl found herself humming and she reached across the table and held the boy's hand as he fished a lump of gristle from his mouth and laid it wet on the rim of his bowl.

Later that night, the girl banked the fire and followed the boy into the back room. As he took off his shirt, her eyes wandered over all his familiar scars. As he took of his pants, she noted his stiffening and his thatch of hair, the hollow of his thigh's socket, the lopsided swing of his purpling sac. She pictured the little book, which she had not gotten down from its shelf in some years now, and what it might have to say about the valves in him that were opening and those that were shutting, the plush and thud of his blood, the intricate flame of his nerves. But that is not what she saw, and that is not what she imagined. When he pushed her back on the bed and fit himself inside her, the girl envisioned her interior spaces as a forest, a field, a marsh, stinking with peat, over which the grey water slid thin as a mirror. Try as she might, she could not see the picture of her ducts and her glands, her flushing secretions, her channels, her folds. Try as she might, the sound in her ears was not a regulated measure of fluids rushing and receding, but the wind in tall grasses and the weird, high call of a hunting bird.

As usual, when the boy was done, he knelt naked in the middle of the room and, as usual, she walked naked into the kitchen to fetch his stick. When she returned, she stood over him, but she did not lift her arm to strike.

"I think I am tamed," said the girl when her boy looked up at her in question.

"Oh no," said the boy. "You're mistaken. You're wild; I'm tame. Remember? That's how it's always been." But he was wrong and, for the first time, the girl lashed out at him to meet a need of her own. She struck him so hard that his ear filled with blood and she heard something crack in the thin bowl of his skull. He was driven to the side and levered himself up on one elbow.

"You see?" said the boy, "I was right," and the girl hit him again: in the mouth, on the thigh. She struck him across the spine and on the hand where she heard his fingers snap. She hit him on the ears, one and then the other, until they lost their shape. When she was done, there was something wrong with the way the boy was breathing. His jaw was off kilter and one of his eyes rolled loose in his skull. He seemed smaller, wetter. "Like a baby," the girl thought, but, strange as it seems, she had only ever seen a human baby at some distance and did not know why this thought came to her now, so unbidden.

She helped him into bed and tore long strips from a sheet she had saved for this purpose, soaked them in witch-hazel, tied up his wounds. What she felt before drained out of her. When she was beating the boy, she wanted to run: to jump through the window and race through the cold town, feel the cobblestones slap against the soles of her feet, feel the frozen clods of dirt crumble beneath her weight. She had wanted to stretch the muscles of her legs until they burned, but now, as the boy turned his head to let her dab at his ears, she considered where she would have gone, what she could have taken. Who would then have had her after what she had done?

"Should I be sorry?" she asked the boy.

"No, no," said the boy, whistling through his broken lips. "You've never been better."

Still, she was sorry, and after this day something between them was changed.

Many years later, the boy and the girl had grown old. Their seasons were spent like any seasons: a steady progression of rains and passing beauty. The boy kept his job at the butcher's shop and the girl saw the children of the first children she taught come again into her kitchen, the ghosts of their parents shadowing their faces as they lay their wet mittens steaming on her stove. Some mornings, they woke entwined. Some mornings, they woke culpable and hurt. The girl found herself inordinately irritated by the way the boy sat with his legs apart, his belly overlapping his groin. The boy often criticized the way she chewed, mouth open, or her inability to describe the measurable goals of her day at its dawn. In short, they were unique only in their habits, and even in the performance of these, the girl felt a sameness settling over her. It had something to do with the inside of houses, the preponderance of doors. No matter which of her students' households hosted the annual spring thank-you dinner, they all had curtains to pull over the windows and fences snug around their yards.

In the town, the layers of the observable world were stacked neatly atop each other. In the forest, they had been fanned in messy overlap. In the town, to truly see, one had to decipher the logic by which the thing had been hidden. In the forest, like on the pages of her book, what was there was laid open in the moment of its working. Nothing was hidden, only unobserved. The forest didn't care how it was apprehended, is what the girl finally concluded. The town hummed with the constant invention of its self.

But, after a certain year, the girl had spent more of her life in one than she had the other. After a certain other year, she could no longer remember what had been so important about being different from the boy. More often than not, she felt full and did not suffer from thirst. She could look out the little window in her kitchen and see something that pleased her: a tethered horse twisting weeds from between her fence slats, a man with a red scarf flaring at his throat, a little bird, white-headed, thrusting out its breast in preparation for a song.

"So. So. So," the little birds sang and the girl also sang that song. In the evenings, she beat the boy lovingly and explored her vast interior spaces. Each time, she went a little further. Each time, she brought back the same handful of sedge-grass and held in her thoughts the same vision of purling white skies.

One day, the town hosted a parade to celebrate the harvest. Every person of the town was expected to march in it, though this was an unspoken rule, and the girl and the boy did not wish to be an exception. For this festival, each townsperson dressed as a symbol of their public life. Those who farmed wore tunics embroidered in rust, moss and gold. They carried wicker baskets overflowing with roots and flowers and the women wove wreathes out of grapevine which they interlaced with their hair. Those who were makers, the blacksmith and the cooper, carried the tools of their craft and their children rolled before them those same tools transformed into instruments of faith or derision. The women who were mothers had built great domes out of melon hulls and straw and carried their bellies once more outthrust before them. The women who stood in the alleys in the late nights when the bars let out wore long tunics pinned all about with bits of ribbon curled like the corners of a scornful mouth and left their own faces bare and clean, pale as mirrors in the bronze light of the day.

The girl spent a long and careful time composing her and the boy's outfits. For the boy, who spent his days in the service of efficient rendering, enabling the magic that would transform the body of a cow or lamb into the body of a stonemason or fishwife, the girl fashioned an outfit made entirely of folded brown paper. She did not cut a single piece, but from the reams and reams the boy brought home to her, she creased and fanned, pleated and rolled trousers with deep cuffs and wide, shallow pockets, a shirt with soft, loose sleeves and a vest which could be buttoned by means of paper buttons slid through paper button holes. She pressed a belt with a paper prong that lay against a paper buckle and folded shoes with a paper tongue, eyelets and laces. Finally, she fashioned a paper cleaver, deceptively light, which had a warm, worn haft and a wicked paper blade, very thin and sharp. Whenever the boy moved he made a soft rustling like someone idly turning the pages of a book. He examined himself in the mirror and turned to her with a face so filled with pride and gratitude, she felt moved to press her hand against his paper shirt and feel the shifting of his heart.

For herself, a teacher, a sayer of words, she had made a different sort of outfit. Out from a drawer in the back of their cupboard, the girl pulled the skins of the rabbits she had stripped and dried over the years. Generations of skins, if one thought of it that way. Mothers and fathers, their children and children's children splayed before her headless, empty paws curled on the table. Of these, she made a voluminous dress stitched so the rabbits' furs in black and cream and sand and pure blind white pressed against her skin. The rabbits' own skins, still marked here and there with the line of a tendon or vein, presented to the world a tough, dry outer layer that hung on her stiffly and resisted her movements. All about her, the empty little paws hung down and as she walked the girl felt the furs brush and rustle against her thighs and stomach like the rabbits themselves, reanimate and seeking from her both comfort and warmth.

Together, the boy and the girl in their parade finery made quite an impression. From their own front yard, they entered the line of the parade as it wound past them and the girl heard the murmurs her friends and neighbors made. Sounds of delight and astonishment, she thought. Sounds of welcome that ebbed around them as she took the boy's hand in her own and walked out under the sun.

The parade was long. It wound up the town's high streets and dove into the low ones. It circled the town hall and marched to the corners of each of the community fields. All around her, the girl saw the people who had bound their lives. There was the butcher's son, who had taken over from his father, wearing a long, white apron, and brandishing a bouquet of chicken's feet. There was the banker who had loaned them the money for their cottage, bent now double with age and pushing before him a wheelbarrow full of miniature houses and barns, flat wooden disks that symbolized fields and here and there tiny wooden babies with their smooth heads painted gold. There were the other girl and the other boy, her long ago students, grown stouter and duller but essentially the same. They walked together but did not touch each other and the girl's belly was huge with false gravity and her skirt was a labor of green and blue feathers sweeping the ground.

She turned to her own boy and adjusted the shoulder of his paper suit. He was waving to people marching on either side of them, eyes slatted against the heat of the blacksmith's mobile oven. She saw how his face had fallen, how his nose had grown. She saw how his eyes were pushed deep in his skull now, how his cheeks had caved into a slide of folds. His ears started red and thick from the sides of his head. "We are old, we are old," the girl thought, but just then the band started up. The boy noted how each of the players were dressed like their instrument and the girl saw a reflection of her formidable dress wavering on the back of the tuba player's helm.

They were there: in the sun, on the hill. There was no denying them, either what they had been or this simple thing they had become. The boy leaned over and said something close to her ear. They had reached the top of the highest hill in the town and here the parade disassembled itself, became a crowd pulsing in toward its center and out toward its fringe. The boy and the girl faced their friends and neighbors. Everyone shook each other's hands, gripped each other at the elbow. Some kissed the air behind each other's ears. The tuba bloomed like bubbles rising from the peat and the crowd turned as one to face the town. The trumpet pealed like a tree cleaving in a storm and the crowd sent up a great, booming cheer.

"To the town!" shouted the townspeople and the girl and the boy shouted with them. From here the girl could see the streets unraveled and the fields unwieldy with fruit in these few days before the final cull. The air was crisp and high—a blue, thin air—and she could see the slate roof of her house like the roofs of all her neighbors. It was so clear and small she felt as if she could reach out and fit it on her thumb like a thimble. Around them massed the forest, patched with sunlight, seeming to stream as the clouds streamed across the sun. The forest like a tide, ascending.

"To the fields!" shouted the townspeople and the girl and the boy shouted with them. Within her dress, the girl felt the furs shift about her. Next to her, the girl heard the boy rustle as he shifted his weight.

"To the forest!" shouted the townspeople and a spell that was cast many long years ago suddenly, finally, broke.

A few hours later, when the crowds dispersed, there was found on the cobblestones a drift of brown paper and a heap of torn rabbit skins. Of the boy and the girl, no trace was ever recovered and, after a short search, the townspeople collectively wrung them from their memories. A minor mystery for the October ghost tour. Nothing more.

There was only one witness able to tell the story. This was the butcher's youngest grandson who had happened to be crouched at the girl's skirts at the time. He had been fascinated with her dress, had the intention of thrusting his finger into the hard clasp of one of the claws to see if it would grip, and so he was close, very close, saw it all. But, though he was interviewed several times by the magistrate, the tale he told made no sense. Something about their bodies shrinking, their empty clothes falling to the ground. Something about two little birds with white caps and bright black eyes hopping from the garments' loose necks and cocking their heads to peer up at him. The butcher's grandson described the sleek line of their feathers, their trim wings. He described how they blinked, the fragility of their eyelids, the moment of blindness when they were most at risk.

For a short time, the birds hopped about the cobblestones on their stiff legs, pecking at crumbs, dodging the revelers' heedless feet. They crossed each other's paths, before each other, behind each other, but gave no sign they were working in concert or were aware of their momentous change. Then, as if at an unheard signal, both sprang into the air, pumping their competent wings, and rose above the heads of their fellow townspeople. They wheeled once, the boy saw them, and flew off in opposite directions with no show of sorrow or even farewell.

"It was as if they didn't know each other at all," the child said.

Try as he might, the magistrate could get no other answer out of him and it was observed that this was a child who had come to his mother late in life, who had been born at the end of a long, difficult labor. His head was too large and round, the magistrate observed, and his hair crossed it only sparsely. His eyes were too wide and his cheeks were too red. Hadn't he been born in the light of a dubious moon? the magistrate said. And didn't these things happen? And wasn't it a shame?

For the rest of his short, baleful life the child was treated with gentle constraint. His bad behaviors were overlooked and his good ones too fervently praised. When he died, his family erected a monument garlanded by lambs, cast a concrete bench for quiet contemplation and fashioned a little fountain to gurgle at his feet. Many years later, when the forest had taken back all the lands of the town, it was still possible to see the outlines of his grave through the tangle of thicket and to apprehend the shape of the bench beneath its coat of moss. Though the fountain no longer bubbled, every storm filled it to running over. In the long dreaming of the season, birds came there to splash and groom.

They clung to the fountain's lip and sung their songs. They lived their brief lives and bore no witness.

The Groomsmen

One day, she gave birth to seven babies. This was a great surprise, the more so because all of the babies were boys. "I am the mother of seven sons," she practiced in the little square mirror the hospital thoughtfully provided. On the table behind her was a vase with a bouquet of pansies her mother had sent and behind that an incredible number of bassinets.

When she brought the babies home her husband said, "Good Lord," and retreated to his study where he sat and looked out the window, gloomily eating a sack of pretzels. For awhile, she walked her sons up and down the halls, wiped their bottoms with rags, threw diapers in the washing machine, hung diapers out on the line to dry, spooned carrots and peas and beans and chickens and corn and mushrooms and pears and eggs into their mouths, sanitized bottles, sanitized pacifiers, washed their hair, washed their bodies, wiped their bottoms with rags, made choo-choo noises and showed them the spoon, spooned carrots and peas and beans and chickens, made a horse out of her knees, made a horse out of her back, hung their diapers to dry, boiled their bottles, boiled their dishes, rubbed a finger over their sensitive gums. Then, her husband came out of his study and gave one of the sons a pretzel. "It won't be so bad," he said and picked up a spoon.

Previously in her and her husband's lives together she had thought of herself as the kind of woman other men would describe as a spit-fire. She understood there was a certain volatile element to her temperament that would be misinterpreted by those who did not live with her as sexual passion. To her husband, it was the element of uncertainty. Would she take the joke or would they quarrel? In public, would she swallow her melancholy or, turning away from the shop window with its rending display of skins and furs, would she go ahead and cry? Perhaps, she hoped, to her husband the uncertainty was also understood as sexual passion. Perhaps when she cried on the street corner and he said, "What is this with you? What is this thing?" he was really thinking quite clearly of the friction of their parts, the cachinnation of their immoderately creaky bed, the humors of their various desires.

Prior to her and her husband's life together, when she did not think of what she was doing as deliberately living a life, she had been confused by the parameters of possible behavior. For example, when she saw something she wanted, say a pair of blue silk panties, or a ring, or a bole of sourdough bread still steaming from its cross, when could she reach out her hand and take it and when must she occupy herself some other way, her hands in her pockets, in her mouth, folding the hem of her shirt? For example, when she found someone to whom she was attracted—by their laugh, or their walk, or their hand on her forearm, rattling her forearm as if it were a bone in a cage—could she turn to look back at them over her shoulder? Could she sweep all the pint glasses from the table, erect and trembling with anger? With want? Could she take their finger into her mouth? Up to the knuckle? Further? More than one finger? Could she try for the hand?

She had often been described as a difficult woman. People said this to her face with the same tone they might use to explain the difference in pricing between, say, the regular eggs and the organic, brown ones; the picked lobster meat purchased by the pound and the whole, fresh lobster still flexing its blue tail in the tank. She took this in the spirit with which it was intended. People also frequently described her husband as her savior. This she was not supposed to hear, but did, and with such frequency that sometimes when she stepped out onto their terra-cotta tiled porch of an evening to listen to the rain fiddling around in the azaleas, she would hear the description of her husband as her savior as a sort of ambient hum in the neighborhood air. It was a blue hum, like the dusk itself. When it got under the sodium street lights it flared briefly green.

Regardless of their histories, both shared and otherwise, she understood her sons as a new beginning for her and her husband. Children are often figured this way—a point along a time-line at which, in sudden confusion or teleological upheaval, everything changes. Her sons felt to her like a reflex. Her response to them was like their response to her when she was inattentive, or blindly feeling about the darkened house at three in the morning, and held them insecurely against her breast. Her reaction to them was to yip a piercing warning cry; her reaction was to nip. In this way, warning and nipping, a large amount of time passed very quickly.

One day, one of the sons called to announce he was getting married. She was sitting right by the phone when it rang, perched at the very edge of a high stool at the kitchen counter, her hands gripping the edge of the kitchen counter as if at any moment she would leap from the stool and race across the room, though she had been sitting that way for twenty minutes at least. As the phone rang she thought to herself, "There is the phone, ringing again," and counted the rings and considered who it might be, always coming back to the sons because there were so many of them and they had various, often pressing, needs.

In the time that had passed, she had kept her figure, had in fact improved her figure through worry and want and the constant silent expression of male desire which, she considered, was only natural in a household of seven sons. Also, it had become increasingly clear that both she and her husband were local celebrities even outside the circle of their regular environs. She was the mother of very many children and in line at the bank or in the poultry section of the supermarket people would look at her, look away, look back at her with the furtive recognition usually reserved for television weather women or white-collar criminals vindicated by some tricky exigency of law. She had filled with a downy, comforting plushness at the breast but had kept her skinny haunches, her runner's calves. She had grown her hair long and it spilled over her breasts and hung into the freezer, glinting a purple-sort-of-russet in the harsh florescent lights, as she pressed the pimpled skin of the chicken breasts and watched their pale blood well and pool.

Her husband, on the other hand, had declined precipitously in bodily health. Previously, he could be described as slender. Now he was gaunt, his chest almost concave, the skin around his lips blue in certain light as if he weren't getting enough oxygen with his breath. He too had grown his hair longer so that it brushed his jaw line, catching in his stubble, or formed a stubby queue when he pulled it back at his nape. The effect could not have been what he desired—he was a fan of Jeffersonian reason, a fan of the body, a fan of the stoic in both study and practice—but his clear tenuousness had done nothing to lessen his physical appeal. Now more than ever, she followed the lingering gazes of women and found them attached to some part of her husband, his wrist or the small of his back, exposed as if by the chance of his movement to both the light and their scrutiny.

The problem of the wedding was a considerable one for her. The colors her son and his bride had chosen were unflattering, the season dull and her role as mother-of-the-groom ill-defined. Her husband began to spend more and more time in his woodworking shop at the back of the house. He was making a wedding gift for the son—a clock fashioned entirely of native woods, the whirring gears, the chimes, the hollow clapper all hand carved by her husband who frequently cut himself with the sharp tools and came in to dinner wearing mitts of white gauze, bleeding through the gauze in patches. It was such a romantic gesture, she became suspicious. It seemed there must be some other kind of union involved, something more desirable and fleeting, but this turned out not to be the case. Even though it seemed her husband could never finish it in time, on the morning of the wedding he rose in a very quiet, silver pre-dawn and went out into his workshop. She too rose and made coffee and, sipping it, listened to the noise he was making—a syncopated clattering, a rising pitch—and watched his shadow move back and forth across the squares of light cast from his workshop windows over the ruin of their sons' childhood sandbox. When he emerged, the clock was mostly whole. It only lacked some of the fine-work which, if you had not seen his plans, you would not know to miss.

Thus, later on the morning of the wedding, she and her husband met each other in their living room. There was the familiar couch, stained from their years of living on it, and there the end table. There the bookshelves and the entertainment center and the many many family pictures, both posed and candid, and the vase she had filled earlier that week with yellow tulips which had now bloomed past their breaking point, some sides drooping to expose the waxy stamens standing dark against their yellow screen. If she looked through the French doors and down the hallway she could even see herself and her husband reflected in the hall mirror, standing together in complimentary grays next to the couch, her husband fiddling with his tie stud, the gaily wrapped gift-box which contained the clock sitting on the end table next to the lamp. Oh, but who were they? She felt so tired now, and it was only the beginning of what was historically supposed to be a very long day. There would be so many different kinds of emotions to go through. She tried to conjure them up in her head: Pride and Guilt, Strength and Providence, Envy, Greed. Through the French doors and down the long hallway her very small face in the mirror flickered through the emotions. Pride and Greed, Guilt and Providence. She thought she looked strange in her steely gray dress which made her hair take on a sympathetic sheen, her shoulders seem mottled, her mouth like a dent in her face.

"What are you thinking about?" her husband asked. It had been a long time since he'd asked her this, but it had used to be a kind of code between them. At night he would say it, reaching under the sheets to rest his hand on her stomach, and she would say it back. "I don't know, what are *you* thinking?"

"I'm thinking about what you are thinking about. What are you thinking?"

"I don't know."

Eventually, they would just echo each other, their voices so alike, and then they would come together, have sex carefully so the bed would not proclaim itself too loudly, and be surrounded in the house by the sound of their sons sleeping, their seven sons packed into all the corners of the house breathing in tandem through the night.

Now, however, the context seemed different and when she said, "I don't know," her husband used her shoulder to steady himself as he wiped a fine film of sawdust off the tip of his polished shoe. He said, "Where are the directions? Are they in your purse?" and together they walked out the door of their house and their figures in the mirror behind them also dwindled, smaller and smaller, then gone.

The night before it had snowed and the world was unmistakably altered as they drove through the town and out of the town, through the countryside and up into the mountains where their son had reserved a mountain lodge for the ceremony. In the town, the snow made her neighbors' houses look like cheerful idiot children. Some of the houses even had hesitant little ribbons of smoke drifting up from their chimneys which made their doors and their windows looked rosy the way an idiot child's cheeks would look rosy if he had stayed out too long in the cold. She wanted to scrub the houses' cheeks, but of course this made no sense and she shifted in the seat so that her dress, uncomfortable beneath her, wouldn't crease.

In the countryside, the snow fell over the fields and hedges with soothing formlessness, but was already starting to be marked, tracked all over with the markings of animals cutting across the wide, white fields. In the mountains, where the trees grew thicker and thicker and closer to the road, the snow took on a blue tinge. It seemed to be hiding from them, moving through the forest alongside their car so that when she looked she would see snow—gullies of it, blue pockets studded with rocks—but when she turned her head to watch the tightening, climbing road, it would be something else: a pacing, a dark movement between the trees. The snow was in the road as well, fresh and deep. Her husband had to drive slowly, tense with concentration, while she turned the dial on the suddenly squealing radio looking for the latest weather news. As a result they were late getting to the top of the mountain, late pulling into the gravel parking lot of the lodge which was already crowded with other guest's cars—parked at desperate, hasty angles as if they had arrived together, all at once, from every imaginable direction—and late climbing the lodge's wide stone steps, the shoulders of her husband's overcoat frosted with a thin layer of snow which was again beginning to fall.

When she and her husband entered the lodge, they found themselves in the foyer, a narrow room planed in rough pine planks and constricted with the cold that seeped in around the door, through the window panes, up through the cracks in the uneven floor. It was empty save for a coat tree hung about with scarves and hats, mittens stuck to its various knobs, and beside it a chair draped with heavy overcoats. Her husband handed her the box containing the clock and added his overcoat to the pile. It was by far the largest and overwhelmed the other coats, its soft grey wool spangled with melting snow like asphodel spangling a secret, luxuriant, ashen meadow. None of the rest of the coats is so beautiful, she thought. In fact, many of them were ugly and strange. Some of them were also very small—diminutive, doll-like coats with too many armholes and buttons fashioned from the carapaces of iridescent beetles. She lifted the hems of the many coats layer by layer. Some seemed to be stitched of leaves and rustled under her fingers and she realized the whole room was filled with rustling, as if a large crowd were talking very softly, each member of the crowd talking on and on, not necessarily to each other, not necessarily intending to be understood. "Hurry up," her husband said. "We're late."

So she and her husband, dressed in beautiful outfits of complimentary gray, one of them, herself, carrying a gay gift box inside of which was a clock that had just that moment begun to tick, opened the wide double-doors at the far end of the foyer and stepped together into a great, vaulted hall. The hall had been set up like a chapel: rows of whitewashed pews down either side of an aisle carpeted with lichens; garlands of feathers in reds and blacks and grays festooning the rafters; a smell in the air like thick, dark incense, like peat moss, like cold soil piled by the side of a hole. It was altogether a startling effect made worse by the fact that the other guests were already seated, all facing the dais at the end of the aisle on which stood six of her sons dressed in gray, the groomsmen, and one son in black who was today taking a bride. The bride herself was also there on the dais—oh, they were late indeed—and she seemed to have chosen an unusual dress. It was hard to see exactly what shape the dress was, it was so unusual. Hard to see, exactly, what shape the bride was even as she turned, rustling, her face covered by the billowing veil—a hoary veil, crackling, vertiginous—to face her and her husband as they stood together in the doorway. The rustling sound increased and the guests swiveled around in their seats to look.

"What are you thinking?" she said to her husband. But it was altogether too late. The chapel was filled with variable shadows, the brilliant cold light dampened by flurries that clumped as they fell past the vaulted windows. Her husband's face wavered in and out of the shadows; drawn, bluing, extraordinary, she realized, but yet the same as all the other faces he had ever had in their lives together. She pictured her husband in his familiar settings, the easy muscle of his younger arm stretched up to grip the doorframe and the way he held his knife to press a bit of meat onto the prongs of his fork. Yes, even in her memories it was still this face—twitching, unsure what to do with its mouth—superimposed over each of the other possible faces as if someone had clipped it out and pasted it messily over the still scenes of their past.

"I don't know," she said, filling in the gap, but her husband paid her no mind. He stared around him: at the chapel, at the guests, stared at the bride, now advancing down the dais to welcome them, and at the groomsmen, his sons, the smallest and shyest raising one sleek paw to wave. He stared at their immaculate suits, their sharp immaculate heads, long brows, fine whiskers, the dear points of their ears and their bright eyes. He stared at their russet fur gleaming in the snow-light that poured through windows, the little puffs of breath that rose from their black muzzles, their sharp yellow teeth as they smiled, all of them, dear sons, smiled at their parents, happy to see them arriving at last, standing together in the aisle, happy to see them looking upon them, the seven sons, the brothers, the singular bride.

"This is a shock to me too, you know," she said. She felt a little peevish now, a little uncertain with the gift clock ticking, the bride advancing and holding out one indistinct, welcoming arm. Her husband beside her suddenly seemed too small for his suit and continued to shrink, dwindled in the aisle. But a number of years had passed for them, too many for their situation to change much now, and she said it in the way she would have said almost anything. What was there left to do but step forward, graciously, into her daughter-in-law's embrace?

A Terrible Thing

No one would have disputed it was a terrible thing. It was a terrible thing. A thing that had happened, that frequently happened to very many people they had individually known and some whom they had known together. Everyone had a story about it. Their voices were hushed. It was not in dispute. There was nothing to dispute. Everyone had something to say.

The same day it happened, they began to update each other. "She's resting comfortably," one of them said to the other. Some of them would not comment. "I heard she took some soup," some of them said to others of them who, leaving the tight group and traveling across the building, went on to say it to yet others who nodded, tight-lipped. Someone had seen an omen. On their drive in to work, someone had seen three crows by the side of the road. Another one had had an uneasy feeling for weeks. Mr. Haslip had nothing to say about any of it, but he was a confirmed bachelor. Mr. Haslip had round eyes, hard as cherries. Many of the women walked around all day touching each other. One would touch another on the small of the back. One would touch another on the hip. The light was very strange. They agreed.

The women there did not sleep easily. At night they turned in their beds and wound themselves into their sheets. Their cheeks were flushed; they breathed heavily. In the cold mornings, everything had receded. Their sheets were cold and stiff as if the heat had gone out in the house overnight. It had already been an unusually cold winter. The women found they were very hungry. They told each other in the lunch room how hungry they were, but they could not bring themselves to eat, no single one of them, and they began to grow pale and taut like candles. Some of the women had husbands and some had lovers. Some of the women's lovers began to hate them, just a little bit. They wanted to hurt them, just a little bit, and that was okay with the women who felt they had fallen somehow out of the order of their lives. This was already the third day. She was still not back to work. "Are you alright?" the women asked each other. One woman took another woman's hands and pressed them to her cheeks. She moved her head all around with the woman's hands on her cheeks, the pad of one thumb on her lower lip, the tips of the middle fingers grazed by her eyelashes. There was a right way to do things and a wrong way to do things. Someone sent an update: she had taken a turn for the worse.

She was on the mend. She was out of the woods. Mr. Haslip was even more an enigma. He strode down the halls with his hands in his pockets. He stroked his long brown hair like a pet. The women could not help but be a little disappointed. Soon, it would be business as usual. Soon, it would be right as rain.

Spring was coming, though the freeze had not broken. Some of the women had dreams in which they all lived together in an ice palace. The beds were made of ice, the chairs and cushions. For food they ate ice cakes and ice apples, ice gravies poured over cuts of ice meat. They looked in ice mirrors. They fixed the ends of their hair with ice combs.

A long time earlier, the company had been young and they had been young. They had not known each other. A terrible thing had happened to some of their mothers, but no one said anything. Somehow their fathers left the house every day and came home every night. Their mothers draped over the rooms like pinticking; they steamed as if they had been left to dry hung over the radiator. This was the way things were. Would no one go back? They did not yet know what their bodies were like. Their bodies took them from place to place. Some of them had bad relatives, bad neighbors, bad friends. One of them was punched on the chin and bit the tip of his tongue clean off. Another put his hand up a girl's shirt and rolled her nipple back and forth between his fingers. Someone stroked himself into strange places. He did not fit. Someone's mouth filled with blood. In their dreams they traded bodies with each other. Everything was very rough and nothing quite fit. They heard themselves saying terrible things. They did not even know they knew those words. Their mothers floated up at the top of the room with their feet dangling down. Their fathers jumped and jumped but could not reach them. In the library, at the ends of the long cool rows, were certain books on the subject, but, though they had read them all, no one could remember what was said. Would no one go back?

The women walk around all day touching each other. The small of the back, the hip, the top of the thigh. It makes all the men angry and productivity goes down. The building has received a new coat of paint. It is a very nice place to work, plenty of natural light. The women put their fingers inside each other's mouths. In the lunch room, Mr. Haslip is eating a cream-cheese sandwich. Where his teeth come together, there is a record of it. There is nothing to be ashamed of anymore. No one would dispute, it was a terrible thing. Mr. Haslip's hair has grown very long. Why has no one noticed this? It lies across his chest like a quick animal. It is longer than that and it lies across his thighs. The women have all grown very tall and distant. They wear gold about their heads as if they were trees with golden leaves. It is hard to see Mr. Haslip's body amid all that hair, but there it is. Mr. Haslip has a beautiful body. It is very threatening. In the lunch room, the women all stand in a line. They really do dislike each other. There is nothing the women dislike more than each other. This is why they are able to be so patient. Mr. Haslip rears up. He is under tremendous mental strain, but he will not tire easily. He is in the prime of his life. It is on everyone's mind, but they have all stopped talking about it. "Oh!" say the women, "Oh, oh, no." They do not mean it. The ones who have lovers wear bruises around their necks like necklaces of plums. The ones who have husbands are also in fruit. If they think a story has to be unbiased, they are wrong.

Finally, she comes back to work. It has been a long time since anyone said her name out loud. When she hears her name out loud she feels like a child again. It is not that she is better, but she is here. She will not go away. Mr. Haslip says she has done a dumb thing, but it is not her fault. Mr. Haslip has grown enormous and cannot be contained. The women find him very fine, indeed, very sweet. She is confused; she does not recognize anything. At home, her husband is waiting with a bowl of soup for her to eat, but she does not want it. She does not want anything. The light is strange.

Around her head are these golden leaves. Overall, productivity has suffered. The women do not say anything now. It is as if they have donated their mouths to a charity. It is as if they are all making one very high noise, so high that no one can hear it. Someone has punched someone else in the mouth. It is broken. It cannot be fixed. Something is bubbling over. It makes a terrible smell. Someone clean it up. Someone clean up this mess, right now.

The Cherry Tree

Everyone had said there was really a very nice quality to the light that would stream, all year, through the windows in her office. This was before she'd taken the job, before it had even been offered; though, from the beginning of the interview process, she had understood the whole event to be a formality. After all, there weren't very many like her in the country. In the world even, if one were to be frank. She was so specialized. And their needs—their pressing, urgent needs—formed such a tight niche.

In fact, she had not been misled. The light that streamed, all year, through her office windows was thick and nuanced. At times, she even found it a little distracting and swiveled away from the two-way mirror, from her computer screen, to pass her hands in and out of its beams, the noises the children made fading to a disarticulated buzz behind her.

In the lunch hour, her colleagues gathered at habituated times in the spacious room that doubled as a presentation hall when the pharmaceutical representatives came to peddle their wares. The room was designed to defy the idea of institutions. Not through luxe carpeting or banks of white, chocolate-scented orchids, as had been the case at her previous place of employment, but through embracing the very iconography of the institutional soul, thus rendering it a null prophecy. This had been explained to her by the Director of the facility on her interview tour. He had used those words, "iconography," "prophecy," though perhaps not in that particular order, and she remembered looking then as she did now up at the raw girdered ceiling of the lunchroom, with its loops of dangling, color-coded wires, and then over to the riveted steel conference table and the hammered steel door with its improbable, thick porthole window and feeling not as hungry as she had just been, not as sure as she was say that morning of all the possible directions of her life.

One thing the lunchroom and presentation hall had going for it was an emergency exit door that could be disabled and propped open. The man who had shown her how to do this was named Anthony. He was a laboratory technician in the Research and Development sector and thus of a much lower professional standing than she but also, and perhaps thus, not inclined to give a hot fuck, as he said, slipping a piece of computer paper between the tiny diode and its sensor and nudging the door open with his hip. "After you," said Anthony and she went, sliding through the narrow space between the doorframe and his chest, hugging the wall where she could not be seen from any of the south facing windows as she accepted a cigarette from his pack and listened to the paper crackle fitfully against his flame.

Anthony wore his lab coat out of the lab, which was a breach of protocol, and filled its deep pockets with a number of stupid items designed, she suspected, to entertain the children if he ever came across any outside of their dormitories, classrooms or other assigned areas. He carried around finger puppets shaped like jungle animals and brightly colored Chinese finger traps and little rubber balls just the right size to fit into a childish palm. Anthony's preoccupation with items designed to keep small hands busy made her suspect he was afraid of the children, at least on a subconscious level, and one day, pressed against the wall on the right side of the door while Anthony pressed against the wall on the left—both tearing up as the spring breeze blew smoke back into their eyes, both ducking involuntarily as a shadow crossed in front of a south facing window—she asked him about his fear, just brought it up as if it were perfectly approachable, perfectly broachable lunchtime chat. Immediately, she was amazed by herself. On the far side of the security fence, a cherry tree was budding in tightly furled profusion and she concentrated on counting its future bloom. One, she counted. Two. Three. Four. Ten.

"I'll tell you something," said Anthony. "A lot of times, with a woman like you, eventually we will reach the point where there is nothing to it but just to put each other up against the wall." She stopped counting the cherry buds and looked at Anthony. He had a long upper lip and a short, fat underlip. He looked at her and scrubbed his hand back and forth over the hollows of his cheeks as if he had made them with his hand, as if he was still in the process of sculpting himself. "I'll tell you something else," Anthony continued. "When that day happens you are going to like it, a lot, but it won't change anything for you and that's why at the end of your story it's always still you. No transformation. No like mystic power or secret identity. Just you. You understand what I'm saying?"

She said she thought she did and looked down at anything, happened upon his lab coat pocket. The nubby arm of a tiger finger puppet protruded over the edge of his pocket like it was waving. Or going under.

"Uh-huh," said Anthony. He dropped his cigarette onto the walkway and ground it out. "I don't know if you do. I'm saying I'm going to fuck you. It's a simple as that." Anthony bent down to pick up the Styrofoam box lid he had wedged between the door and the frame as a prop and motioned her in front of him. As she edged by, he reached around her and grabbed her breast, found the nipple through her blouse and her bra and twisted it hard. She gasped and Dr. Rutgers looked up from his turkey club and waved. That afternoon she stood in a reticulated lozenge of light in her office window and counted all the buds on the cherry tree. One hundred and sixty-two, she determined, though the angle was not clear enough to ensure perfect accuracy.

Some time later, she was pressed against her window and noticed the cherry tree was fully immersed in its own foliage. It looked preoccupied, but, she supposed, so do we all. She, for example, could not recall what its blooms had looked like in the height of its season, whether it had been a good year for the tree or a disappointing one. She considered asking Anthony, but he was working hard. He put his hands on her hips to steady himself and worked harder, hurting her, really digging in. Behind them, on the other side of the two-way mirror, the children were being led in some sort of song. They were getting the words wrong, she suspected on purpose, and laughing about it, laughing and laughing. The children's laughter sounded spiny to her—brittle, harsh with edges—but perhaps it was only this way because of the quality of the light which today was even more than usually resplendent, falling as it did over her breasts and then beyond them, paying attention to all the details.

Listen

At the end of her life she found herself quite alone, living in an unfamiliar neighborhood on the outskirts of the city. To make a little extra money she rented out her basement as an apartment. A girl moved in and complained about the lack of light. A young couple moved in and fought over who would clean the bathroom. A middle aged man moved in and walked naked through the back garden at night, moonlight clashing on his grizzled chest as if striking off metal. His cock rose just to the height of the poppies and brushed them one by one as he strolled. She imagined it smeared with pollen.

Ah well, she was not unattractive, nor was she old. It was just that her life had turned out to be one without a lot of room, but she did not know it. She had every reason to expect this was a phase: this isolation, this lack of sleep. Every week she got the scale out from its hiding place under the bathroom sink and marked her weight on the long column taped to the bottom of the drawer. She found her bones aesthetically pleasing and, as they became more assertive, she felt as if she was wearing herself—her wrist like a bracelet, her collarbone molded on her chest like a band of sculpted silver and somewhere beneath the jeweled pendant of her heart. Yet, when the weight came back, as surely it would, she thought that too could be a sort of assertion. Her rear, for example, mounded like the graceful back of a Queen Anne's sofa, the meat of her arms like the tasseled fringe of a hassock and her plump feet like little pitchers, one for cream, one with a silver spoon for scooping out the sugar. All of her life had been a series of phases. First she had looked like her father, then her mother. First she had sucked the fingers of her right hand, then she smoked long brown cigarettes that made the air smell like spice and dirt. She would be a body and next, who knew?, a house. So it went.

But then, her tenant moved in. And then, she saw him at night, as she stood in her window smoking and considering the night blooming flowers, walking naked in the garden with his hands clasped behind his back. From there it was really a very fast progression. What did they ever say to each other? She couldn't remember. Just, one night, after she had watched him for a long time making his rounds, he turned to face the window she was standing in and gave her a little salute. He ran his hand through his graying hair at the last moment so somehow it seemed a gesture he would have made regardless—saluting the house, saluting the moonlight sulking in the copper guttering, saluting her as well because she happened to be there, watching.

She considered him, framed by the thickly flowered catalpa, an evening primrose blooming moony at his knee. He had long hair caught into a queue at the back of his neck and a lantern jaw which made his head seem slung forward, made him seem always lost in thought. She could see his previous body, his younger one, through the skin he now wore, muscles relating in competent affinity with the pads of fat that swathed his shoulders, ribcage, abdomen, hips. His legs were still corded and tense, the muscle cutting a heavy groove over his knee as if he were used to frequent lifting, and, though it may have been a trick of the moonlight, his cock looked un-gnarled, smooth and thick, arcing up toward his belly with none of the strenuous yelping sort of fervor she had become used to. They were very different. She knew that right away. He stood in the garden and watched her calmly with a conversational sort of air as she took off first her dressing gown and then her tank-top, as she hooked a thumb in the waistband of her panties and stepped out of them. She stood there with her hands at her sides, palms dishing in the moonlight, and watched him watch her ladder-rack ribs rise and fall, her nipples pucker like sour buds in the cool air, her concave stomach pulse slightly with the beat of her body beneath.

He was his body and she wore hers. She felt embarrassed, like she was cheating, and even went so far as to reach up to her shoulder as if she would suddenly find there a sort of snap or clasp to unlatch. Of course there was nothing, but the next night when she came to her window and took off her gown, her top, her panties, she showed him she had stripped the polish off her finger and toenails, had shaved the sparse fur that grew between her legs, on her thighs and calves, forearms, in the blue hollows of her sockets, and washed and washed and washed her skin until she shone a cold tallow candle in the window, unlit. The next night, she came to the window wearing a gray knit cap and when she had removed again her gown, her top, her panties—her hand lingering there to show him the skin, how smooth and slick it was—she took off the cap and showed him her skull. An unsuspected vein throbbed thickly over the fragile bulge of her temple, and she ran a finger over the weird ridges of her brow to show him that there too she had removed the sparse, thin hair and now stood as close to herself as she could get.

He seemed un-phased, absentmindedly caressing a spray of pink phlox that bobbed against his thigh, and the next night when she came to the window he wasn't there at all. She was unprepared for how she felt at his absence. Before in her life she had occasion to be disappointed, angry. Once she had even become so wrathful, so powerful, she struck out at a lover, catching him by surprise and splitting his lip. Then, watching the blood slick his chin and flow over his fumbling knuckles, she had felt overwhelmingly contrite, had sunk to the floor sobbing and clawed at the back of her neck with her nails. Now, standing before the garden—somehow empty despite its cacophony of buds and blooms which massed riotous even in the grayscale of night, the dark huzzing thrum of seeds and sprouts, tendrils, shoots roiling behind a bubble of silence—she felt stung with rage, wrung with it. A hive of rage striking and striking until all of her was riled, all of her roused, until she was barely contained, striking about her dark bedroom as the moon cast warped shadows on the walls, beating her limbs against the walls, the floors, the mirror where she reflected a blasted, seething heave of bone and shadow, skin and weird, refracted light.

But she did not know him. Not even his name, which she had never quite heard, or his business. He paid her in cash, bills clasped with a thick clip and folded into an envelope he tucked into the space between her screen and her door. Every month, she took the bills and slipped the silver clip back into his envelope, left it for him at the top of the stairs that led down to his basement door. Every month it came back to her the same, so, until now, this was all that had passed between them: the clip, the envelope creased along its lines until it felt like skin, weathered, soft with age. She had no right to her rage. He had no right to his desertion.

She exhausted herself, slunk into a corner panting like an animal. Her head hung down almost to the floor and from her mouth slipped strings of saliva, thick and sour, which she watched pool on the old pine boards of her bedroom. Her eyes were full of blood; her ears beat with it. Her teeth felt newly cut, sharp as a mink's, but as she lifted her forearm to her mouth to test them, she heard a noise, a rapping, coming from under the coiled rug she kept at the foot of her bed.

It was him, tapping at a hatch that had once served some arcane purpose (coal cellar, root shoot) but now connected their rooms. What a detail! How remiss of her never to consider it before, though she had spent hours in a delirium of half-sleep, her bones aching, pressing her febrile cheek to the cool floorboards and listening to him beneath as he paced. He rapped again, this time sounding more like a question, and she threw back the rug, strained to lift the heavy trap door by its iron ring. He helped, pushing from beneath—she sensed his strain through the boards, his arms corded above his head like an Atlas heaving aside the globe—and when together they flung the hatch open he looked up to her, his lantern jaw thrust eagerly forward as if he were about to speak. What would he have said? A greeting? A declaration? His eyes were sunken, dim. He blinked.

At another time in her life she might have seen herself as he did. Or she might at least have tried, glancing in the mirror which gaped a shocked oval directly across from her, and she might have been ashamed of herself. Certainly her mother would have been ashamed of her, her childhood friends, her former lovers. Her father would have been horrified, pushed past speech. He might again have died to see her there in her extremity, her wildness. But this was the very end of her life, its final months, and though she knew almost nothing of the world, she was still animal enough not to waste her time. She pounced.

In the end, sad to say, she was quite violent with them both. She spidered over him, a fury of limbs, and her skin so pale that where he gripped her, pried her, pressed her to the bed, his hands left no mark, only a slight compression as if he had gripped a length of cold wax. She scoured him. She used her nails, her teeth. Where she could not find purchase, she dug in under his shy pads of fat. All over his body she left great welts, thready scratches beading with blood as if he had come through a forest of nettles. She did more besides. More and more as her little dark room filled with that compressed silence (a silence that somehow swallowed their breathing, his moans, her sharp fox cries) and outside the garden roared and trembled, trumpeted, disclaimed.

The garden mustered all of its dense, bushy conglomeration, from the dormant border mums to the fetid corners of moss, from the thickets of wandering Jew and bell-sprung hosta to the cyclamen beating its mewling blooms against the panes of her glass. It mustered its whole self to a hysterical frenzy, a shrill, mouthless clamor so total and extreme that her next door neighbor, smoking a cigarette on his porch and watching the streaming branches of the catalpa toss against the moon, wondered what it was that could have snuck through her fence. Something large, he thought, or several things, cats perhaps taking advantage of the clear night to mate. 'Time to make more cats,' he remembered, some distant line of poetry, and smiled, pleased with himself and this beautiful night. How still it was. How mild.

Their affair continued in much the same way for many weeks. Some nights, he would come to the hatch in her floor and scratch there. Some nights, she would fling it open and call down into the darkness. All throughout he continued to make his garden rounds and she continued to stand for him, a beacon in the window but lighting nothing, guiding nothing, noticeable only because behind her was a darkness so black it seemed a living thing, pressing its furred weight into all the crannies of the room, folding around her like a cloak or a curtain. What did she see during this time? Often it seemed as if she were blind. And what did she hear? She heard a dense roaring, a hum approaching and receding, sometimes a twang as if of a wire snapping beneath an unbearable strain. She did not eat. Her spine now looked like a watch chain and her rib-cage a pocket watch left carelessly open, slung over the back of some chair. It was all new, strange, howling, but sometimes it felt as if there was something—a resonant ache, a stretching—that she had always felt, that she had only forgotten for some little time after she had been born. When they were finished, she would take him limp into her mouth and taste all that was there. The salt and the pearl-seed musk, the copper tang (hers? his?) and under it the bitter yellow smear of pollens. The sex of the lily, the poppy, the rose.

One day, a departure, she opened the hatch herself and descended the ladder into his rooms. For some time now she had been aware of herself in a different way. She felt a fullness, an uneasy shift. That morning, she had woken to the sunlight climbing in tentative inches up her quilt, motes of dust distinctly glimmering against the eggshell walls, and thought, "Ah ha." She had gripped the hasp of her pelvis and shaken it as if in confirmation.

The ladder seemed very long, or maybe her body was shorter than she was accustomed to, curled in on itself. Her dressing gown, which she had thrown on for some reason over her shorts and her yellow Pearl Harbor tee-shirt, flapped about her ankles and threatened to slip beneath her feet, tripping her. Her hands ached, her arms ached, and when she stopped to catch her breath and wipe the sweat out of her eyes, she saw the wall before her had gone from brick and mortar to raw, clay earth, packed and smooth as if shined by the pressure of long use. She braced herself on the ladder with one arm and picked at the dirt, digging a little hole with her forefinger, but all she discovered was more of the same. The passageway seemed much tighter than it should be as well, but she didn't trust her balance enough to turn around. A warm breeze came up the tunnel and fluttered her dressing gown, soothed the backs of her thighs, flirted up the leg of her shorts and out the baggy gap of their waistband.

She found him in his kitchen frying an egg. He was fully dressed, which was something of a shock to her having never seen him in clothes, and seemed pleased to see her, though clearly quite surprised. He fussed over her, settling her in a chair, turning up the flame on an oil lamp he kept in the center of the table. His house was very dark, though all through its rooms breezes of varying temperatures floated and crossed as if about them were countless invisible passages out into the open air. Shadows, too many it seemed to her, shifted on the prettily wallpapered walls of his kitchen and she tried to remember if this was a paper she had chosen herself or something he had added. And this room, hadn't it once had a window? A window obstructed by the tangle of a forsythia bush which her first tenant, that miserable girl, was always threatening to raze? On the far side of the room something massed in a way that might suggest branches, but then it didn't seem to matter anymore. Then, she didn't care.

Would she like an egg? She would not. Did she mind if he ate? She did not. He poured some tea for them both out of a steaming kettle and sat across from her, merry, his jaw thrusting after his eggs and toast in a ruminative fashion as he watched her drink. His clothes were very simple—blue jeans, a black tee-shirt that flattered his shoulders—but they unnerved her. They made him seem like someone else entirely, someone with a name she should, by now, know. He sopped the last of the yolk off his plate with his last bite of toast. She sipped the tea, a bitter musty tea, and shuddered as a breeze flipped suddenly up the back of her neck.

She said, "I'm pregnant."

He froze. His mouth fell open, revealing a yellow smear of yolk in a way that she found very comical and she snorted with laughter. Then he reached for her across the table. His hands cast great winged shadows on the wall and the light of the oil lamp skewed the proportions of his face, making his eyes seem huge and dark, his mouth a wet hole. Oh, but he was delighted! She had never seen him happy like this. He laughed. He came around the table and knelt at her feet, reached for her stomach with one hand, gripped her thigh with the other. Laughing, his mouth was wetter, his eyes hidden. She looked down at the top of his head, his face buried now in her lap where she could feel the hot gusts of his laughter. His body seemed to hulk in its skins, in his *clothing* she reminded herself, and it shook and quivered, his hand pinching up her thigh, his mouth wet against her stomach, kissing her kissing her, hot and wet. A baby! A baby! A baby!

"I will not have it," she shouts. She stands, shakes him off. The room seems to contract around her, a ring of muscle tensing. It is dark and hot. She cannot see; she cannot. "I'm getting rid of it. I will not have it." Because who is he, after all, to be so pleased at what she has done and what she will do next? She presses the top of her skull with her fingers and imagines her belly the same shape, with the same tensile glow. She imagines her body going on and on without her, building something, massing itself to a terrible effort and she left alone in her dark room, incidental. She drops the teacup and it breaks in half on the floor like the two sides of an egg. Scalding tea leaps up against her leg and around her in the whickering shadows something moves very fast. Inside herself, she feels a deep, irrevocable tearing.

All that follows next happens in darkness. She wakes in his bed and he is kneeling beside her, a washcloth in his hand. She wakes on her hands and knees in a tilted hallway (her hallway? behind that distant door, her bath? her mirror? her robes?) and feels a wetness between her thighs. When she puts her hand there it seems to come away sticky and green. She wakes to his face, concerned. His face, alarmed. His wet eyes, his strange expressions. What is the sound of his voice? She wakes to a pressing pulse, on all sides a tightness as if all the space in her is being squeezed out. The light is red, pounding. She wakes and she is alone, out in the garden. It is night and very still. High above, the moon is a sliver, so white it is almost translucent, almost not there at all. Her body feels wrung, each muscle stretched and sore as if she has gone through a tremendous struggle, but when she tries she finds she cannot lift her head, and when she concentrates she realizes she cannot feel her arms and legs. At the center of her is a great hollowness. A wind comes up and from the corner of her vision she sees the spiteful poppies toss their heads.

"I have been stepped on," she thinks. "A boot has come down."

Already the insects have found her. Next to her, something dark and shapeless unfurls and begins to cry.

Many Things, Including This

When she stopped looking around so much, everything got a little better for her. For example, previously on her short drive to work in the mornings she would look to one side and see the ambulance men parked in the drive-through eating their egg sandwiches. To the other side, she would look and see a group of school children all wearing unseasonably heavy coats with oversized fur-trimmed hoods. With the hoods pulled up the children looked like ecumenical bears, gathered together to consider questions of portent and consequence. Hoods down they look skinned, raw. Perhaps they were waiting for a bus? Every day she drove past too quickly and was concerned for their safety, then hers.

A little further on, still looking around, she might see a hawk perched severely on the Baptist church steeple; a Giant Sale banner snapping loose of its eyelet and rippling on the wind; a waft of plastic flowers blown from the cemetery to the bustling gas station across the street; a woman in a pink skirt taking very long steps.

Previously, when she went out at night, she would continue this behavior, looking at the bartender and the booths, at the people in the booths, the shadows behind the people, looking at the corners, back and forth from corner to corner until she was no longer sure which way she had come in. She had headaches and body aches. She had mind confusion and confusion over the ordinary things outside of her mind like house keys and terra-cotta pots. She was capable of looking back and forth between a green shoe and a stand lamp, a chicken breast and a tea pot, a cassette tape and a thick, blue pen, a loop of wires and a bundle of lilies for hours and hours. Clearly, something had to change.

At first, she did not look around simply by not moving her neck. There remained the question of her eyes, but in less time than you'd think she had conquered them too and stared only straight ahead. She had always been told she had beautiful eyes. They were an uncomplicated color, demanded very little from their audience. If one were lost in her eyes it would only be for the afternoon. Nothing to panic about, nothing to report back on. With her new way of holding her neck and her straight-ahead eyes, people seemed to find her disconcerting. They looked at her eyes and looked away, looked and away, looked and away, each time a little more startled, more angry. Under her gaze, people developed a tendency toward extreme agitation. They would fidget and pluck at their clothes. Soon they were hopping from foot to foot like apes. They hunched their backs and threw their arms up into the air exactly like apes, but of course she did not know this because she did not look. For awhile this was the perfect solution and many things fell into place in both her emotional life and in her career.

Then, her boyfriend, a recent acquisition, began to complain that there was something different about her.

"What is it?" she asked. They had gone out to dinner and she was eating a plateful of mussels. She could hear the ligaments creak as she pressed the shells flat and she held each mussel up before her eyes and studied its saffron sheen. She was a little worried about eating a bad mussel—this was not the best restaurant and they were far from water—but each one slid into her stomach and settled there in a wholesome, briny, companionable way.

"I don't know," her boyfriend said. "Maybe it's like you're thinking about something really awful. Something that if I knew about it would make me uncomfortable and ashamed. Maybe it's like you're doing it on purpose. I don't know." Her boyfriend looked down into his soup. Across the restaurant, a band was setting up on a little raised stage and they crossed back and forth through her vision carrying cables and amplifiers, guitars and drum-sets, accordions and a kazoo.

"I'm not thinking of anything," she said. "I'm thinking about mussels."

But her boyfriend said, "I wonder what kind of music this is going to be," and turned in his chair so all she could see was the back of his head.

Later, they decided to go ahead and have sex anyway. It turned out the band had a large local following and the restaurant quickly filled up with people who passed drinks over her head and dipped the edges of long, embroidered scarves into her boyfriend's soup. The mussels were not off, but still she felt like something had happened. She had just a bit of fogginess around the edges of her mind and didn't feel up to trying the thing her boyfriend wanted to try, not right then, not without some time to think through the logistics.

"It's okay," her boyfriend said, "just get on top." But then the bed began to make an unpleasant noise and, because she was looking at the wall directly above the headboard, she noticed they had chipped the paint a little there and after all this was a rented house.

"Okay," her boyfriend said, "I'll be on top." The situation became awkward. The bed continued to make its noise and one of the pillows had been carelessly arranged so that it kept falling down over her eyes. Her boyfriend went on for a while, much longer than usual, and when she pushed the pillow back so she could see the place on his neck which she liked, she noticed the vein that usually beat there so steadily was swollen and erratic in a way which was clearly indicative of stress.

Finally, her boyfriend rolled over and lay next to her. Together, they looked at the ceiling.

"I wish you would just stop thinking about it," he said.

"Thinking about what?" she said, but he pretended to be asleep.

The next morning, she got up while her boyfriend was still sleeping and got ready to go to work. She brushed her teeth and looked at her eyes in the mirror. She chose her shoes by touch and ended up with alligator pumps, which would do just fine, and left very quietly, locking the door behind her to keep her boyfriend safe.

On the way to work she looked only ahead. She saw the road which had recently been repaved and glistened a little. It was an unusually foggy day and the sky pressed against the road in a way that made its newness more noticeable and the particular oldness of the sky, by comparison, a cliché. The road had been repaved so recently—it occurred to her it must have been in the night while she slept—that the road crews had not yet painted the abrupt yellow dashes and strict yellow lines which would normally tell her how to go, so she centered herself in the middle of the street.

Straight ahead the street was like a lavish, glistening tongue—unhealthy, too full of itself—and the sky was the low vault of a pallet afflicted with some kind of cottony disease. She decided to take a break, though she was almost to work, and pulled into the gas station for some gas and maybe a Danish to eat after lunch. When she got out of her car her alligator pumps made echoing taps against the ground. The fog here was much thicker and she concluded the gas station must be situated in a natural depression. She could see only the roof of her car and then, when she turned, the pump directly in front of her. Even the trash can and windshield cleanser stand had been reduced to vague outlines and the gas station itself was invisible except for a neon sign advertising a brand of gum which glowed red through the fog. CHEW SNAP said the sign and suddenly she realized she wasn't alone.

Looking straight ahead, she couldn't see who had joined her. She sensed there were many bodies and assumed a kind of density and compactness to the bodies that was confirmed when something padded jostled her arm.

"Who is it?" she said. "Who's there?"

But there was no answer.

She asked again. "Who is it?" she said. "Who's there?"

Her voice sounded to her as if the fog had somehow gotten inside her throat. She couldn't tell how far it had carried, if it had carried at all beyond the chambers of her throat, and wondered how she would ever have been able to tell this. What was the empirical standard for how far one will be heard? And what, in that same vein, is the furthest limit after which one will no longer be heard? In other words, she thought, what are my boundaries? What keeps me in?

"Who is it?" she said for the last time. "Who's there?"

But it was the children, of course. And, as there were a great many of them, she was quickly overwhelmed.

A Category of Glamour

In the nineteenth year of her abandonment, Penny Linden began to talk to the man in the garden. This was not the first time Penny had seen the man. She could not remember exactly the first, but a series of images came readily to mind when she considered the issue: a figure fading back into the deep cool underneath the pine trees, the shadow of a bowler hat falling across the inset patio sundial. These were from the early years of Ollie's absence, before she began to consider it abandonment. No one else's husbands had come home. Later, the man in the garden became more precise. He was tall. He wore a neat gray suit, somewhat old fashioned, and a bowler hat which Penny considered an extravagant eccentricity. The man carried a walking stick and his hair waved in a lush, oiled way that made each curl seem purposeful and intent. One curl unspooled neatly in the center of his forehead and the man brushed it aside with the back of his wrist as he stooped to inspect the bell of a foxglove or tap a loose patio tile with the tip of his stick.

When Penny first met Ollie he had curls too, but they were tight and held close to his head like a fleece. It wasn't psychologically difficult for Ollie to shave them off because they were so close to his head and so tight they did not seem like separate expressions of his body, but more like a helmet, something that could be removed at will rather than amputated. Ollie had to shave them off to fit on his real helmet. "There can be no room between the skull and the helmet, except for padding," he told Penny. She thought later she must have found him dashing saying that, holding his helmet under one arm while the evening sun drowned in the whiteness of his head and neck. The rest of Ollie was bronzed from hours of drills on the base, then weekends at home with her in the garden. There was something menacing about the whiteness of his head and neck. It was like a weapon and Penny felt sorry for all the enemies he would swoop down upon bearing that whiteness.

At that time, they were putting in a vegetable patch. Ollie had a book with many facts about vitamins and minerals. The garden was to be organic because Ollie's book also had facts about pesticides and pictures of malformed infants which Penny looked at in the kitchen at night after Ollie had gone to bed. In one picture, the little boy had been born without a face. Where his face would have been was an expanse of shiny skin, like a hardboiled egg, unbroken except for two slits which Penny assumed were his nostrils. The rest of his body was perfect except for a blank, smooth place where his genitals would have been. "Oh, now," thought Penny, eating a sour organic tomato over the sink and looking at the picture. "Now, that's going too far."

Ollie planted marigolds around the vegetable patch to discourage the fire ants and he saved eggshells from breakfast, crushed them and mixed them with the ashes from her ashtray. Then he dissolved that mixture in water and sprayed it over the soil around the plants to keep off slugs. He made another water soluble solution out of cayenne peppers and sprayed it on the tomato plants to protect against worms and deer. "You shouldn't smoke," he told Penny, "but if you are going to, at least there is a useful application of the product."

After Ollie was deployed, Penny took down all the maps of Northern Africa that Ollie had framed and hung in the living room for her to reference while he was gone. She traced the continent's outline with her finger and then blew smoke on it. She put the maps away in a drawer and went into the kitchen to lean against the sink and look out at the garden. Fireflies floated up between the tomato vines and she smoked a cigarette and said to her stomach, "You go right to hell." It was an experiment, but she wasn't sure of the hypothesis. Inside her, the baby was a round, self-satisfied stone, like a river stone that has rolled in the water for a long time without tiring of the sport. "Go right to hell," Penny said again and laughed with the baby who pushed up under her hand like a stone kicked from the bottom.

After Ollie was deployed, Penny had to think of things to do for amusement. For a while she tended the garden. She had a large straw hat to wear. She also had a leopard-print cowboy hat. The cowboy hat was fuzzy and thick. Her mother had bought it for her as a joke when Ollie was transferred to the Alabama base, but Penny wore it sometimes in the garden. It made her head sweat and cast a terrible shadow across the sundial. At that time, Penny's shadow was always terrible, so lumpy and full of unexpected demands. Still, she would not turn away from herself and when she stood on the sundial path to find out with her body whether it was one o'clock or closer to one thirty, she was not bothered by the shadow that seemed to move through the pine forest behind her.

After Max was born, Penny began to go to the grocery store for amusement. Max rode in a cloth sack that Penny could tie around her neck. The sack was designed especially for babies and had holes through which Max could dangle his legs. It was blue and on the front, picked out in lemon and navy stitching, was a large, yellow duckling who was saying Qvack! Qvack! and flapping his stubby wings. The baby sack was another gift from her mother and Penny was disturbed by the singularity of the duck. Was it supposed to be a stand-in for the baby? For any baby? Were a baby and a duckling actually the same thing? This seemed possible to Penny. Max, at least, looked like no one she had ever met and she could imagine calling him Bear or Black Snake with equal ease, but it didn't seem polite for the sack to point this out so publicly. There was also something unsettling about the duckling's insistent Qvack!, but Max seemed to like the baby-sack and when they walked down the aisles of the supermarket he reached out toward the shiny cans of peas and white potatoes and tiny ears of corn.

In this way, many years passed. Penny let the vegetable patch overgrow its marigold border. She neglected to make water-soluble cayenne mixtures to spray on the tomatoes and when she planted in the spring she did so by filling a plastic bag with mixed seeds and tossing them wildly into the air. The garden gave way entirely to ornament. Fat, striated eggplant grew up among the pansies. Cyclamen and violets trembled in the fierce shade of a pepper bush. The sundial path, which Ollie had lined with butterfly bushes and silky lamb's ear, was overgrown by a rampant sweet pea vine and the wrought iron numbers were gentled by a thick layer of moss and made useless by the prevalent shadow of sapling pines.

After the fourth year of Ollie's absence, other women's husbands began to come home to the base. Penny would hear the parade for the husbands winding down the road past the house and when she put Max in the car to drive to the grocery store she had to turn on her wipers to clear confetti from her windshield. That same year, she began to attract cats. They seemed to like the garden and many of them would come across the fields and over the hot road to lie in the cavernous hollow of her forsythia or stretch out on the patio tiles. Most of the cats did not like the house, or Penny, but some would come inside and then went in and out as they pleased through a little swinging flap Penny installed in the bottom of the kitchen door. Penny named the cats that would come inside things like Mulligan and Cooper. The names were interchangeable and she did not distinguish any one cat from the number of cats who padded through the kitchen or haunted the forsythia waiting for birds to come to the feeder. The only cat Penny consistently recognized was a yellow tom with a missing eye who she called Qvack! Qvack! and let sit beside the sink while she did dishes so he could consider the faucet water. Occasionally, Qvack! would dip the tip of his paw into the faucet's stream and then shake it in the air above his head. He would look up at her with his one eye as if sharing the results of this experiment, or asking her to take a note, and Penny would rest her thumb between his ears.

Also in this time Max grew older. He did not like the cats and shut his door quietly against them at night. He also did not like the grocery store as much and began to find his own ways to amuse himself. Once, Penny came home with two bags filled with shiny cans of baby carrots and found Max in the living room with all the maps of Africa and the shifting Mediterranean spread out in front of him. He had stolen one of her cigarettes from the pack she kept on top of the refrigerator and was smoking it while he examined the maps and wrote the names of countries and their major rivers on a sheet of paper. All of the country names and river names listed neatly together looked very attractive to Penny. She thought of the great, pink gums of a hippo she had seen in a magazine, the hippo yawning in the river, its stubby peg teeth streaming water. She was going to tell Max about the hippo—how it too was in order, was free not to concern itself with what came next—when he turned around and saw her in the door with her bags, Qvack! sitting next to her and touching the back of her calf with his tail. Instead, Penny said, "You shouldn't smoke a cigarette in the living room, Max," and went into the kitchen to put the cans away. That evening, sitting in the garden, Penny thought that now Max did look like people she had met, though which ones and under what circumstances remained a mystery. He also looked a little like that boy with the hardboiled egg instead of a face. Penny considered that knowledge until it was very dark in the garden, but not so dark she couldn't see a shape bending over the bed of verbena, or smell their sudden wounded scent as the figure clipped a bouquet and held it up to his indistinct nose.

One day, all the men who had been on Ollie's mission were home. Many had come in time for their parades. Some had arrived for more somber processions, the headlights on their processional cars overwhelmed by the blazing summer light of the fields and road, but all had reported for their accounting. Penny imagined the list she knew existed somewhere on the base. It was not a long list, no more than three pages, but it was tidy, squared away. Each name was followed by some fact or other, except for Ollie's name which, Penny felt, had all along been unfactual, bare.

There had been a series of phone calls, by turns both official and silent, from the base to Penny and from Penny to the base. Finally, an officer had come and sat on Penny's sofa with his knees held tightly together and his hat placed precisely on top of his knees where he could hold it without appearing to be holding anything. "I'm sorry, Mrs. Linden," the officer had said, "but we will have to assume." The officer was not very old but had bands of gray hair that bristled elegantly at his temples. Penny supposed that she had met his wife at a potluck somewhere. She had a faint impression of Spanish rice and pigs-in-a-blanket, a very tan woman with lip-gloss in an unfortunate shade of tangerine. "This is still a human business, Mrs. Linden," the officer had said. He cleared his throat a few times and stroked the top of his hat with his index finger. "Sometimes the only thing left to do is assume."

Penny had invited the officer to stay for dinner. "We are having a macaroni casserole," she had said, "It's my son's favorite," but the officer had already placed his lovely hat on his head and straightened up by the door. "I am very fond of your hat," Penny had said and the officer shook her hand for a minute and looked over her shoulder at Max who was sitting in the corner. When he was gone, Penny sat on the sofa with a tall glass of limeade. Max went into the kitchen and came back with his own glass and a bottle of gin. He poured some gin into his limeade and held the bottle out to Penny. This was the summer Max was sixteen and in the dusky light that slanted through the blinds his face looked stretched and fervent. Penny found herself always wanting to touch his forehead to check for a fever.

"I think you have to put it in the oven before it actually counts as a casserole, Mom," Max had said, crunching an ice cube. He poured some more gin into both of their glasses and later got up and turned on a lamp.

Another day, Penny came back from a trip to the store and mistook the house. She drove past it in one direction and then again in the other before turning around in a neighbor's drive and counting the telephone poles to her own gravel driveway. In front of the house was the familiar crab apple tree with its hard, green apples. The house itself had a familiar rainspout pulling away from the roof, a familiar missing brick crenellating the chimney. It had the architecturally significant turret that many base wives had commented on standing on the walk with their empty casserole dishes or leaning against their husbands in the post-potluck dusk with a half empty bowl of guacamole balanced on their other hip, saying, "Well, I hope it's a girl. She'll live up there like a princess," while the cicadas emoted from the tops of the surrounding trees. Eventually, though, it was Penny herself who lived in the turret. She moved Max's crib up against the wall and later, when he slept alone and through the night, Penny repainted the funny ducks and piglets onto the walls of the master bedroom downstairs so Max could have more space. She didn't feel like a princess, but the turret looked out on the garden and the pine barren behind the house. In the mornings, Penny would wake only when the light crested the tops of the pines. She would stand in the window of the turret watching the wind sweep through the tips of the trees like a hand carelessly raking through hair.

It was the turret that finally made Penny decide she was in the right driveway, but the house itself was an entirely different color than when she had left that morning. In the morning it had been a chalky antacid kind of blue that faded into the blue morning shadows and was peeling in places to show its elemental brick. Blue with black shutters. Now, the house was a creamy peach with bright green shutters. It looked like the lovebird Penny had often admired in the pet store window in town. The bird had bright, vacant eyes and terrible, wise feet. Sometimes, Penny would go in the shop and the owner would let her put her finger in the cage for the bird to grip with its foot while it admired itself in its little looking glass. Penny thought there was something about the lovebird's peachy head and bright green mask that made it look like a baby, a poor baby all dressed up by some mother who had purchased too many cute hats. The bird liked to sharpen its beak on a cuttlefish block while it held onto Penny's finger and at such times she was swept away by a complex series of pleasures and the pet store owner would ask if she needed him to hold her purse.

For a long while Penny stood in front of her house and considered its new colors. She shifted her bags—what heavy bags, she could not now remember what was in them—and observed the shadow of the ladder leaning up against the front of the house elongate rapidly across the lawn. Finally, Penny opened her front door and went into the kitchen with her purchases. The kitchen was surprisingly bright and noisy. Max was sitting at the table with two other young men drinking beers and smoking. They had music playing on the radio and all three were laughing at once as if at the end of a long, hard-earned joke.

"Mom!" Max said, standing up and stretching his arms wide as if introducing her to the kitchen. "What do you think?"

"What do I think?" said Penny. She lined up three jars of borscht and a little tin of sardines. Qvack! jumped up on the counter next to her and nuzzled the plastic bags.

"About the house, what do you think about the colors?" Max said, coming around the table and turning down the radio. "I thought it was time for a change."

Penny rolled back the sardine tin's lid with its little tin key and offered one to Qvack!. He accepted it graciously, eating it in two compact bites and licking the fish oil off the counter with only a trace of shame. Penny considered her son. He was leaning against the doorframe, stretching easily to grip the lintel. He hadn't shaved that morning, or it was late enough that the hair had grown back, and the line of his jaw was underscored by dark stubble. She thought about the nature of gifts, who they were most important to. Her mother was very inclined to buy hats, but had never once come to the house in Alabama where they had moved and then settled. In Penny's turret closet there were dozens of prim hat boxes tied at the top with lush, wrinkled ribbon.

"It's lovely, Max," Penny finally said. "Very lifelike." Max grinned and swooped away from the doorframe, turning back to his friends with his arms spread wide again as if introducing them this time. Here is the kitchen, his arms seemed to say. Here is my mother and her one-eyed cat. Max turned the radio back up and Qvack! put his paw on the back of Penny's wrist and miaowed politely for another sardine.

Max's two friends' names were Jenner and Paul. They were house painters and Max was also going to be a house painter and drive with them in their blue truck as they circled the town looking for houses in stages of ill-repair. Penny sat with them at the kitchen table and listened to the radio while Jenner talked about small business owner's insurance and ladder length and latex over-coats. Paul was more the silent type and Max, sitting between them, eventually suggested they go down to Newt's for the drink specials and a local band. After they left, Penny took down a pony glass from a high shelf and mixed herself a limeade and gin. She stood in front of the cupboard for a long moment and then reached up for a second glass. She opened the back door and, with Qvack! running out in front of her, took both drinks into the garden.

It was almost dark, an uncertain moment in the evening that made the garden seem longer and narrower than it ever appeared in the day, and Penny watched the ground carefully to avoid tripping as she made her way to the little garden bench which sat underneath a pecan tree. Honeysuckle had grown up around the legs of the bench and over its back. When Penny sat down she sank back into its dark, fragrant tangle. Penny swept a few empty pecan shells off the bench next to her and took a sip of the limeade. She called out, "I've brought you a drink," and watched as a shadow detached itself from the nearest pine trunk and made its way over to her.

The man in the garden bowed slightly to Penny, sweeping off his bowler hat in a gesture that seemed at once both extravagant and restrained. He took a seat on the bench next to her when she offered, pulling up his gray suit pants at the knees and unbuttoning the front of his suit-coat, and sipped the limeade and gin.

"This is not at all unsatisfactory," the man in the garden said after a long silence. His voice had a curiously thick quality to it, as if he had only a moment before been eating spoonfuls of yogurt and honey.

"It's only limeade," Penny said. The evening light was catching in her glass, making the limeade glow with an unsettling luminescence. She could see the man in the garden's socks where his pant legs had risen above the fine line of his leather shoes. The socks were a light pink, tastefully flocked in charcoal. His shoes were highly polished but marked by a water line just above the sole and over the toe, as if he had been standing a long time in damp grass.

"Just so," the man in the garden said, "but you'll forgive me if I don't say I find it delightful. Adjectives tend to overstate the moment, don't you agree?"

Penny did not know whether she agreed or not, but they sat for a long time together and conversed while the last of the light slowly died out and fireflies replaced it with their drowsy, intermittent glow. When Penny finally went into the house, she stood at the sink and rinsed their glasses. She tried to remember what they talked about, but could only remember the fireflies and the scent of honeysuckle, another muskier scent and Qvack! purring at her feet. The man in the garden's glass held an imprint of his lips along its rim, as if his lips had been filmed with a fine gloss, and Penny touched a finger to the impression. She held the glass up to her face and inhaled deeply, but all she could smell was the tang of limeade and a faint, bitter trace of gin.

The next night, Penny brought drinks into the garden again and the next night after. Soon it became a ritual to sit on the bench and watch for the man in the garden's shadow solidifying from the deeper bank of the forest's shadow, to listen to the crisp rustle of his suit as he settled himself on the bench. One evening, Penny went out as usual and found the man in the garden already waiting for her on the bench with a little silver drink cart pulled up next to him. The cart held a variety of carafes and mixers and a plate of finger sandwiches, crusts removed, which seemed to pull all the evening light into their white squares.

The man in the garden rose as Penny approached and bowed his customary, elegant bow. "I thought I might repay your hospitality," he said, expertly pouring her drink into a cut-glass tumbler and proffering the plate of finger sandwiches. "I find an evening snack a fine fortifier for spirits of all sorts, wouldn't you agree?" he said.

"I do," said Penny, taking a bite of the sandwich which tasted airy and green. "I do, I do."

Penny began to spend longer and longer evenings in the garden, often staying until the trunks of the pine trees began to grow gray and individual in the pre-dawn light. No matter how long she and the man in the garden sat on the bench, the liquid in the carafes never seemed to go down and there were never any fewer finger sandwiches on the plate. Yet, when Penny woke up in the morning, sometimes now sleeping into the afternoon, she felt clear-headed and relaxed. Only very rarely did she stand at her turret window and watch the wind rustle through the tops of the pine trees. The garden in the daytime seemed graceless and foreign. Its colors were garish and seemed to Penny as if they had been chosen out of a catalogue, pre-ordered from a set.

Max was also staying out later and later. During the day, he painted houses with Jenner and Paul. Sometimes, he would come home for dinner and Penny would suddenly remember that she had forgotten to eat all day and would pull together a macaroni casserole. They would eat together at the kitchen table, listening to the radio and talking a little, but Max was tired and spattered with paint. He would have paint in his hair, flecks of blue or gold, and paint in long streaks down the backs of his hands. He would have paint on his face and Penny wanted to smear it down along his cheekbones and over his jaw, but the paint was always dry and flaking. After dinner, Max would shower and go out to Newt's with Jenner and Paul and the girls they met there and danced with. Sometimes, Max would tell her, "Eat, mom, eat. You never eat anymore," or that there were letters for her piling up with the mail. When he came home, Penny would watch from the garden as the light in his room flicked on and his shadow crossed in front of the window. She would watch his window after the light flicked off, but never for too long.

One night, Penny and the man in the garden were sitting in their usual spot having their usual drinks. Qvack! was stretched out next to the drink cart purring in the lingering heat that radiated from the patio tiles. "The summer is getting on," said the man in the garden, taking a slim brown cigarette out of a silver case he carried in his waistcoat pocket.

"Yes," said Penny, though it seemed to her that nothing had changed. The flowers were various shades of gray in the night garden, but they were all still blooming in their random, fervent bloom. The honeysuckle that immersed them didn't seem to have progressed at all in its conquest of the bench.

"Yes," said the man in the garden and sighed languidly. "So too all things, don't you find?" he said and offered Penny a cigarette. As they sat together and smoked Penny heard the rattle of Jenner and Paul's blue truck as it pulled into the driveway. She heard the door slam and Max's voice as he called "Goodnight," and something lower, more indistinct. The light in his bedroom flicked on.

Penny watched as Max's shadow crossed and recrossed the bedroom window. The light flicked out and Penny took the last sweet sip of her drink, holding the glass out to the man in the garden who unstoppered the carafe in perfect anticipation. Suddenly, another light impinged on the garden and Penny looked up, startled. The kitchen light was on and Max was leaning into the window, cupping his hand to peer out at her and the man in the garden sitting on their bench. He seemed to be very far away and the light in the kitchen cold and clinical. It made his features harsh, Penny thought. His brow was too severe and his skin washed-out, an unpleasant white.

"Oh," said Penny, and her hand jerked a little, almost spilling her drink.

"Ah," said the man in the garden, "this must be your son. Max, is it not? Your son, Max?"

"Yes," said Penny. She recovered herself and sucked the few droplets of spilled liquor from her finger. "That's Max. Would you like to say hello?"

The man in the garden recovered his bowler hat from the bench next to him and put it on as he rose. He bowed toward the window and swept the hat down over his heart with a little military flourish Penny had not seen him use before. "Hello, Max," he said and inclined his sleek, curly head in greeting.

But Max did not respond. He continued to peer out the window, leaning closer now. Penny thought the light not only made him look severe, but also featureless. She noticed he needed a haircut. His hair as it hung around his face made his head seem overly large, misshapen, and he was leaning in such a way that she couldn't see his body, only a vague, contorted suggestion. Max rapped on the glass sharply with his knuckles. He turned away from the window and switched off the light. The man in the garden turned to Penny and lifted a quizzical eyebrow.

"I'm so sorry," Penny said, half rising herself. "Normally, he's a very polite boy." Penny thought about it and could not remember whether Max was normally polite or not. It seemed to her that he wasn't, but the man in the garden sat down on the bench and put an arm around her to help settle her back in her seat.

"It's quite alright, my dear," the man in the garden said. He was leaning close to her, peering into her face with an expression of kindly concern. Penny could smell the faint sweet scent of his breath. It smelled like grass, as if he had been grazing in a meadow, and she thought his teeth, which she had never particularly noticed before, seemed very large and square and white. "We are all so young," said the man in the garden, looking over her shoulder and into the unmitigated darkness of the forest. Then he laughed.

The next day, Penny woke late in the afternoon. Qvack! was sleeping curled at the foot of her bed and the light as it poured through her thin curtains seemed brash. Max was standing in the doorway.

"I've been calling you for a long time," he said, frowning and pushing his hair back from his forehead. "Do you have any idea what time it is?"

Penny raised her arms above her head and stretched. The sheets rubbed against her nipples with a pleasant friction and she realized she was naked. It didn't seem to matter though and the light hurt her eyes. She sat up in bed and shielded her eyes from the window.

Max turned away and stared at his feet. He kicked the edge of her braided rug so it flipped back over itself and then smoothed it flat. "Anyway," he said, clearing his throat and then stopping to clear it again. "There are more letters for you on the table. They look important. Official. I paid the bills." He turned and started down the hall.

"Max," Penny called after him. She heard him stop in the hallway. "We need to talk about last night."

"What about last night?" Max said. From the way his voice sounded, Penny knew he still had his back to her.

"Well, you were rude last night, to my friend, and that is not how you're supposed to be. That's not what I taught you to be."

"Jesus, Mom," said Max and Penny heard the creak of the top stair as he started down.

Penny rolled onto her side and pulled the sheet up over her shoulder. She rolled a little further, onto her stomach, and wiggled until the mattress pushed her breasts apart and to the side of her ribcage. The sheets against her stomach felt cool and heavy, thick. "That is not what you are for," she called after Max.

When Penny got up later that afternoon the light was already starting to thicken in golden rectangles across the floor. She stood in front of her closet looking at her clothes which hung in orderly rows above the hatboxes. Finally, she picked a thin, cotton shift, a slip which she had bought to go beneath summer dresses. It didn't seem to fit right, so Penny pinned it at the back with a line of hatpins. Max had already left for the evening. His dishes were piled in the sink and he'd run water over the plate which made the smears of ketchup and hamburger juice run pale and oily just below the surface. On the kitchen table was a stack of thick letters in manila envelopes. They were held together with a rubber band and Max had left a hot-pink Post-It note on top of the stack. It read: *If you don't open these, I will.* Penny unstuck the note and pressed her finger to the adhesive seam. She pulled the envelopes one by one out from under the rubber band and spread them over the table. The stamps were dark and thickly banded by cancellation marks. The letters had gone many places and been marked by them. Penny held one of the envelopes up to her nose and inhaled. It smelled like paper.

When Penny went into the garden that evening, the drink cart and the little plate of finger sandwiches were standing as usual by the bench, but the man in the garden was nowhere to be seen.

"Hello?" Penny called and looked around. The garden was getting darker earlier and the bowers of scuppernong and heavy honeysuckle vine were in complete shadow. The forsythia bush hulked a dark, unblended outline. Penny found herself grinning, an uncontrolled expectant smile, and strolled down the dark path toward the bench. "Hello?" she called again and the garden seemed to echo her. On the bench where she normally sat was a tented piece of heavy, ivory stationary. On the front of the stationary her name was written in a fine copperplate, but when Penny picked it up she saw nothing was written inside. Qvack!, who had been following behind her, croaked a rusty miaow and rubbed against the drink cart, causing it to rock slightly on its wheels.

A wind picked up in the forest and bent the tops of the dark trees toward the garden in a formal sweep. The pine trees tossed, creaking deep in their limbs, and then the wind passed into the hollyhock beds, chiming their silent bells, rustled through the nodding poppies, skirled a thick patch of creeping morning glory and lifted the hem of Penny's shift. The wind whipped the cotton shift around Penny's legs and slid coolly over her knees. She laughed and raised her arms, twirling a little as the wind suddenly flattened her skirts to her side and then died. When she turned to the bench again the man from the garden was standing behind it watching her.

"A place setting," he said, nodding toward the ivory stationary which Penny still held. "I thought we could stand to be a little more formal, don't you agree?"

"Certainly," Penny said, still laughing, though the sudden absence of the wind made the garden seem very still and quiet.

"Also a gift," said the man in the garden. He came around the bench and presented Penny with a bouquet he had been holding behind his back. He bowed low before her, holding the bowler hat in place with one hand and presenting the flowers with the other. All Penny could see of him was the long, sleek line of his spine, the impeccable suit coat expanding slightly with each breath.

"Thank you," said Penny, taking the flowers out of his hand. "They're lovely," she said, though to her the flowers seemed slightly aggressive. They clung thickly to their stems and drooped over the edges of the bouquet in long tendrils that hung and swayed against her wrist. The flowers tapping against her wrist reminded Penny of a moth tapping out of the darkness against a lit window, insistent and softly destructive.

The man in the garden straightened and stood looking at Penny. He was silent and serious. Penny noticed his eyes, which she had always thought were a precise shade of blue, were really a dark brown. They were almost black and the man in the garden blinked slowly, his long, curling lashes resting against his cheek. "The summer is almost gone," said the man in the garden. He took the bouquet out of Penny's hands and laid it on the little bench.

"Yes," said Penny, "you've said that before." She took a step closer to him, then another and the man in the garden pushed his bowler hat back on his head. A single curl unspooled itself on his forehead and Penny touched its tip. The curl bobbed and the man in the garden reached out to Penny and pulled her, for one quick, close minute, against him. Then, just as sharply, he stepped back, hissing and shaking his finger. He had pricked his finger on one of the hat pins that lined the back of Penny's shift. The man in the garden held his hand up between them and he and Penny both watched the bead of blood swell and break, trickling down his long finger and into the palm of his hand.

"Careless," said the man in the garden, "Wouldn't you agree?"

"Yes," said Penny, and the man in the garden reached out and brushed his finger over the front of her shift. His blood was black in the dark garden and marked her dress. "Yes," said Penny, taking a step closer, "I would."

When Penny came downstairs the next day, Max was gone again. The envelopes on the kitchen table had all been opened and one of the chairs was lying on its side. Penny sat the chair upright and opened a fresh tin of sardines for Qvack! who was sleeping in a patch of sunlight on the kitchen counter. Sheets of notepaper were spread over the kitchen table. They were filled with cramped handwriting on both sides and had been creased many times. Some of the pages had drawings on them: little figures of men and animals, an airplane, an ocean, something that looked like a single, unblinking eye. Penny dumped coffee out of Max's mug and refilled it with water from the sink. She stood over the kitchen table and sipped the water, stirring the pages around with her finger.

Qvack! jumped down from the counter and trotted into the living room, his tail held high, burbling a question. Penny looked after him and saw that the front door was standing open. "Careless," said Penny, and flicked the edges of the white cotton shift around her legs. She went to the front door and started to shut it, humming a little tune that kept floating through her head. It was a cloudy day out, dim and shifting, and Penny noticed the crab apple tree's leaves were starting to turn. The small leaves were flushing red and yellow along their veins. The bigger ones were already curling brown and heaped around the tree were soft, pitted apples. Bees hummed over the apples and Qvack! sat on the porch twitching his tail.

Penny hummed the last of her tune and started it again from the beginning. The shift, she thought, was the best of all possible dresses, but it was getting a little cold outside, making her legs feel stiff and thick. Suddenly, Penny realized that the tune she was humming was also now a tune she was hearing. It was bigger than the version in her head, full of brass and a heavy, thumping drum, but still the same song and getting louder. Penny stepped outside and down the porch stairs. She went around the crab apple tree and to the end of her walk. A wind picked up, rustling the dead weeds by the side of the road and sending a line of yellow poplar leaves spinning through the still, expectant air. Penny stood in the middle of the road and looked down it. Far in the distance the song gathered strength and form. A trumpet rose in a triumphant tinny spiral. Cymbals crashed and rung and crashed. Penny shaded her eyes and looked at the cloud of dust rising at the end of the long road. She watched the dust, which could be a parade or any other type of thing, as it traveled toward her.

A Beautiful Girl, A Well Loved One

Then, one day, she went into the forest.

This was a surprise to no one. What is the surprise when a girl comes to no good? Maybe how is a point of interest, maybe when.

She was an only daughter, much beloved, and beautiful by all accounts. Her grandmother, who doted on her, said she looked just like her mother when her mother was that age. Her mother, who had a long, disfiguring scar fissuring her face, said she had unusual coloring, should always make the best of her coloring, pay attention to the light, pay attention to warming fall tones, stay away from blues, particularly ice blue, and also her hair, what nuanced hair!, people would pay good money for hair like that, people did. Every year, the girl's grandmother would tell her she looked just like her mother at that age, until one year she didn't and from this the girl surmised the age at which her mother received her ruinous scar. It was younger than she had expected. Many things were left unsaid between them but the girl was a child, beautiful and beloved, and the house they all three shared back then was so small there was nothing to do but sleep tucked together like spoons, trading places over the years as the grandmother shrunk and the girl grew and the mother wiped her one weeping eye over and over with the hem of her skirt.

You might know something about biological imperatives. You might know something about hive societies, or nesting dolls. Perhaps you have a treasured memory of a kiosk on the banks of the river Volga, fingering a coarse wool shawl, pressing your lips against the cheek of a porcelain girl, very rosy cheeks, a real girl's hair, a skirt you can flip and discover beneath the head of a wolf or a pig who then has a skirt you can flip and discover beneath the head of a girl. Perhaps you are inarticulate. Perhaps you are dogged by an intermittent fever, your life marked by tremor, or perhaps you are unusually tall and feel as if the world was modeled for another sort of mammal entirely, another sort of girl. You see, I make assumptions about you even as I avoid them. You see how foolish it would be to tailor this story toward your tastes. I cannot help what happened. I would not want to.

Of course, it is often the case with girls that they must make their own way out into the world and from there find their own way back. The more organized ones draft maps or make hatch marks in the trunks of trees, bend branches, leave a patter of crumbs. Sometimes a girl will tie a thread to something she wants to come back to and dole the thread out behind—a raveling hem of her cloak or the loose end of a golden ball, very precious, she was previously using to string the geese in a row to and from the lake. This is why if you come across a thread in the forest you should never pluck it, not even rest your fingers upon it, or the girl it belongs to will feel it quiver and come rushing back—her hair in a tangle, her mouth so frightful, stained with berries—to see who has crossed her trail.

You see, there is a reason for everything. If you wait long enough it will all come clear, but in the meantime many things change.

For the girl, so beloved, she got a good job. She was used to being petted but also used to going without, and this unusual combination prepared her for the corporate world. Up, she went, up and up. Each of her offices was more spacious and more naturally lit. In each office she was allowed to keep an increasing number of personal mementos—a picture of the grandmother on the bookshelf, a wooden spoon, nicked at the edges with years of teeth, balanced atop the computer console. Always there was an office above her which made her feel safe, beautiful girl used to small spaces, and clear at least about the direction in which she should go. With the money she made she bought her mother lace hankies. She bought a house in the suburbs, a condo in the city, kept the old tiny hut in the country and sometimes drove past in her red car—an old car, restored, a powerful engine, flattering bucket seats—and noticed how the yard grew wild, the trees bowed wild, the vines came tangling up and every year the little hut was harder and harder to see from the road. She had enough money. Not so much she couldn't spend it, not so little she had to count it penny by penny and keep it in a stocking tied to the foot of the bed. She had plenty to eat and wore fashionable clothing in warm fall tones even in the summer when the sun clanging back and forth between the windows of the tall glass buildings that surrounded her condo made a terrible racket for the eyes. At night the girl would sit on her balcony and drink a cool drink out of a slim glass. She would call her mother and her grandmother, who were now living in the house in the suburbs, and compare with them the sound of the cars hooting at each other many floors below to the sounds of the suburbs: crickets and cats, knives scraping the faces of china plates, spoons rattling in empty bowls, brushes ripping one hundred times through crackling tresses and the tiny *skirt-skrit* of something living in secret inside of the walls. They all agreed that everywhere was very loud. Each place was, in fact, almost the same place because it was so loud, and this made them feel close to each other and closer to who they had used to be in their old house in the country when the girl was a child.

But what does a girl need? She needs a skirt, of course, a good pair of shoes. She needs something to apply to her lips and another sort of thing to apply to her cheeks, such rosy cheeks, something to give the appearance of warmth even when the girl herself is cold. And what does a girl want? All manner of things. It would be difficult to list them even if you had the time, which you do not, you yourself being so busy, and the girl herself also so busy acquiring items she needs to make her seem warm. A brassier for her breasts, razors for the fur that grows in her creases, a cigarette to hold at the fold of her lips, another cold drink, many colors, sipped from the throat of another slim glass.

The girl, so beloved she had to hang up on her grandmother's breath every time, sat on her balcony overlooking the city and had another drink. The city's natural colors were pink and lime green, tan, roughly various, and a teal that flared at unexpected intervals. As the sun went down, molten in the tall buildings' cacophonous glass, pink and lime, tan and teal sobered, muddied each other, dipped in and out of the canyon alleys where they seemed to become a dusky kind of gray. This was a nightly display in all seasons, and the girl appreciated its constancy but did not overdo it. She poured herself another cold drink. Some nights, she called back inside to the man who was there and he joined her, sitting across the latticed iron table from her, admiring the colors and the failing light, admiring her—although he did not overdo it—while she admired him until they stopped seeing each other and saw only each other's most admirable parts. His jaw line, for example; that funny thing she did with her mouth. Some nights, she called back inside and the man wasn't there. Some nights, he preferred to remain in the living room with a book, or at the kitchen sink washing the faces of each of their dinner plates with slow, lascivious gestures, gazing out the kitchen window onto the various tan bricks of the building next door and their startling teal shadows.

You too might have a man in your home to whom you can call over your shoulder. Perhaps he is also the sort of man who washes your dishes; also the sort of man you lie next to in the early morning as he snores and you reach over to scold him, reach over to scold him, do so until he springs from the bed and goes to squat in the bathtub, naked, shivering with anger. Perhaps you fight. Perhaps you hiss at him and batter the overstuffed arm of the couch with your fists to show your man what you could do to his body if you let yourself, for even a moment, really just let yourself go…Perhaps you no longer recognize yourself. Perhaps even in your man's most admirable parts you no longer recognize how your parts used to fit. Perhaps when you look in a mirror— also in the bathroom, the tepid water running to cold, another problem with the heater, your man, shrunk-pricked, still angry, asking "Why, *why*, do we have to have this fight now?"—you see a simulacrum of a person: dough-hole sockets, slung-dough jowls, the mouth a cavernous gawp, yawping, yawping, the eyes trapped and furtive. At this juncture, many girls choose to set forth on a journey.

But what does a girl *need?*
A basket. A ball of string.

Sooner than she would have suspected, the girl came to believe her looks were fading. There was a looseness around her mouth, a thin scrim of fur above her upper lip. There was a line furrowed between her eyebrows and a scar she could not remember receiving white and spidery on her temple. It was the scar that bothered her most—a thin, crazed, complicated scar like cracks in porcelain glaze. She tilted her head under the bathroom's harsh globe lights and observed herself from all angles in the mirror. She handled herself the way someone might handle a pot unearthed unexpectedly in the garden, thumbs brushing the crazed glaze, rolling it between the palms. How long has it been there? Why was it buried? Observe, the only thing holding the pot together is the weight of the dirt that has filled it. Accidental dirt, perhaps some incidental treasure—silver spoons, photographs with singed corners, a complete collection of teeth, tiny as seeds, drifting through the strata of the soil. She went into the bedroom and asked the man, reading in bed with a cat asleep on his knees, if he had seen her scar before, if he remembered how it had come to her. And he mistook her. He heard the girl say, "Look at this scar, you gave me this scar," and he was angry. It became another sort of night altogether—the book left tented, slipping from the foot of the bed, the cat arching disconsolate in the windowsill—and in the morning the girl packed a brief lunch and went for a drive in her old red car in order to clear her head. There were many roads she could have taken. Some led deeper into the city: twisting roads, maven roads, the rough walls leaning closer, the turns curling always to the right and people pressing their ears to their doors or thin plaster walls to listen to her passing, listen to the whisking rustle of trash in her wake. Some led away over a high ridge and guttered down in dusky hollows, lavender dust spuming in twin tails from her tires, the road skirting a cliff and the sea like fields of thistles, each field collapsing below the next field, purple-cone thistles, their glassine stalks. The sea like a flower, her car like a horse, the road unfurling like shoots on a vine. These are only the echoes of a story.

Of course, we all think in complicated ways. Even the least of us, even the meanest, our minds are busy and tense. Of course, there was only one road for her. She thought without thinking and turned the wheel under her hand. There was a basket in the passenger seat, a little dirt shifting, drifting from her ears, black scrim under her nostril. A little room was being made, a little hollow.

When she arrived at a place in the road that felt right, the girl parked the car, shouldered her basket, set off into the forest.

What do you see?

> I see the forest, the trees, their pale bark. I see a path which is rutted, grown over. Flowering mosses I can't bear to crush.

And what do you do?

> I follow the path, skirting the mosses. I come to a pitcher, drink from the pitcher. Come to a key, pocket the key. Come to an animal...

What sort of animal?

I can't see. It's dark. It's like there's a hand pressed over my mouth.

Aren't you a silly thing? Didn't I warn you?

Whatever it is, I watch it feed. After a time, it moves off into the forest—a shadow of a shadow—and I follow, first tying one end of my string to a branch so, should I desire it, I can find my way home.

Why have I wasted so much of my time with you?

I hear the animal breathing. The crack of the twigs as it breaks its trail.

Are your ears full of potatoes? Is your head full of sand?

I come to a pitiful clearing, a doorstep. I see a house the forest has invaded, nests on the lintels, a tree grown through the roof. I run out of string and tie the end of my line to the doorknob. The animal's mark is fresh on the stone.

Why, foolish girl, should I bother to save you? Why, stupid girl, should I unlimber my axe?

I am a beautiful girl, a well loved one. Inside, I hear breathing. I open the door.

The Silent Woman

There once was a woman who swallowed a fly.
I don't know why she swallowed the fly,
Perhaps she'll die.

When Mary was only thirty she met a ghost. She was in one of those places people go when the people who have to attend to them every day are required to send them somewhere, for whatever reason. In her case, it was because she had swallowed a fly that had gone on living inside of her. This was not on the official paperwork. Almost nothing was. Rather, Mary supposed, she was there because she had become indefinable and lived the sort of life in which being defined was quite an important prerequisite.

The facility was in a northern state, ringed by frequently mist-shrouded mountains. The winters were assumed to be fierce and uncompromising, but she had arrived in early summer and all of Mary's surroundings seemed to be struggling cheerfully out of the ground. There was a garden and a quaint, ramshackle barn in which the staff kept four nanny goats and a spavined pony named Bert. The garden was lush and impractical, zealously attended by both staff and residents alike. It was bordered to the west by a fast, shallow, tea-stained river that chucked gamely along between its high banks and spilled over the old millrace with a companionable show of foam and spray like someone laughing too loudly at a party. She had a private cottage composed of an airy south-facing bedroom, whose window boasted an assertively framed view of the mountains, and a tidily furnished sitting room. There was also a half-bath with a toilet, sink and shower stall in which the management had thoughtfully included a little cedar bench. So the ladies among the residents would have someplace to rest the ball of their foot as they shaved, Mary concluded, though it did not escape her notice that there might be a more dreary rationale. The residents were not all so young, after all. Some of them were actually quite decrepit or, unlike Mary whose fly buzzed in her throat and made her scintillate, fizz at all her joinings, were so denuded by their official diagnoses that they might need some kind of moral support, if only in the form of a cedar bench, to get on with the duty of sloshing hot, soapy water into all of their stultified crevices.

"No kitchenette, I'm afraid," said Jolene, the staff member who had given Mary her tour and helped her settle into the cottage. "You understand."

And Mary did. The knives and such. The oven. This was a facility, after all, she explained to Jolene who nodded and showed Mary the button to push on the call box if she needed assistance in the night. A facility, not a vacation, Mary emphasized. And what a relief that was! If there was one thing Mary had had enough of it was vacations. The stickiness, the enforced levity. The spiraling panic as the last day approached and one realized afresh that one had not yet swum out past the sandbar, or hooked an infant shark from the pier. She remembered one year in particular when she was very young in which her father had insisted the entire summer that the low concrete dome just visible across the bay from their beach house porch was what he termed a rainbow silo. If she watched it attentively enough, he insisted, she might be the lucky girl who saw the rainbow first, just as they unleashed it and before the colors had separated, so it would appear to her, lucky lucky girl, as one big band of astonishing light. Well. It had been his idea of parenting, she told Jolene, who was clacking along in her brown clogs, leading Mary to the community dining hall for her first lunch. He really was the most uncomfortable father and she was an only child so there was no one else on which he could practice. She supposed she understood the impulse, the paternal bonhomie which he must have believed was patrician in some sense, as obsessed as she knew him to be with the trappings of the Republic, but really. Really?

The dome had turned out to be a sand bunker, Mary told Jolene as she left her at the door. A place where the city council kept backup supplies of pillowy white sand dredged up from ocean trenches and bleached sterile to replace the dunes washed out to sea or carted off in the treads of dune buggies and the tight rolls of beach towels. But, even after she knew the truth, she had never been able to shake the feeling that the empirical evidence of her failed observance proved she was not after all a lucky girl. Not, it turned out, special in any particular way. And wasn't that something a parent might be expected to foresee? Of course she didn't feel that way anymore, she told a member of the kitchen staff as he levered a sliced chicken breast onto her salad. She had grown up. A lot of things had happened. And now here she was: resplendent, didn't he think? Mary turned on her heel to show him the full affect and, from the murmuring room of residents intent on their meals, somebody clapped.

So it went on from there.

It soon became clear to Mary that the facility, like the rest of the world, had broken itself down into two groups which could be roughly defined as the Haves and the Have-Nots. Mary had always disliked the imprecision of this term. Have what, after all? The answer was almost never as quantifiable as money which could be stacked and counted, double-checked for errors. Rather it implied some amalgam of various moneyed signifiers, attitudes and ways of holding one's wrist cocked and languidly vulnerable as one swirled one's drink in its glass, which shifted from epoch to epoch with infuriating fluidity. Even in the very short epoch of her own, Mary's, life! The eighties, for example, in which she had observed her older female cousins decked out in beguiling pastel blouses and high-waisted cotton trousers that showed off not only their waspish waists and slim, tight hips, but, more subtly, the firm, plump placard of their lowest abdomen. This advertised a sort of invulnerable vulnerability. A cool, juicy quench the men of the party, boyfriends and male cousins and even the uncles who, when drinking, were not totally surreptitious about their admiration of each other's daughters, clearly longed to drain. Mary remembered looking down at her own body, absurdly banded by the shadow of the blinds, and wondering how her own pallid, hairless cleft could possibly metamorphose into such grandeur. Surely it would have to be replaced, she concluded. An operation that she was not yet old enough to know about in which the frog-like thing she had now would be cut out of her and a new sort of thing—sleekly pelted, waterproof—would be stitched firmly in its place. That was a sort of Have which Mary could understand. She wanted those pants, to be what was inside those pants. She Haved-Not it.

And then, just when she was old enough to procure them, and to realize how foolish she had been to think any part of herself could be lifted away—she was stuck with all of it just as it had first become her in the warm slush of her mother's womb—the fashion changed and to Have became not to show. To appear to Have-Not through cheap fabrics, coarse patterns, clothes that competed with the girls' bodies with their sullen clangor, and thin white scars that laddered up the inside of the girls' forearms like a public tally of the passing days. It was frustrating. Mary was an early riser and had plenty of time in the morning to devote to costume. She was unfulfilled by merely tousling her over-bleached ratty curls and ringing her eyes with thick, black liner. When she was with a boy, a boyfriend or a pick-up or, more than once, an older male cousin on the basement couch, the back of her car, the floor of his bedroom, a blanket in the dunes, or under the pier, she couldn't help but think as the boy ground on top of her and thrust his ruddy, strenuous penis in between her tight lips and into her shockingly deep interior vacancy that the whole experience would be enhanced for her if only first he had had to strip her out of those pants.

But, as the facility was meant to be a stripped down, more simply codified version of the world from which the residents had all sought refuge, in this distinction as in so many others the lines were more clearly drawn. At the facility, the Haves were what Mary's friend Donovan termed, "the decorously insane." They were allocated private cottages and no night-time supervision, though when they entered their houses after midnight the doors would lock irrevocably behind them and not let them loose again until breakfast unless overridden by the emergency sensors which were attuned, one assumed, to fire and other natural disasters. They were also allowed free run of the facility grounds (garden, river, barn, spa, meditation parlor, yoga studio, dining hall and community greenhouse) and daytime access to the surrounding town which offered two Laundromats, a grocery store, a shop of healing herbs and crystals and a gas station that sold an impressive variety of spirits.

Doctors Throng and Bledsoe, who had founded the facility and remained its chief psychiatric practitioners, operated under the guiding premise that the most pressing part of a life was the experience of it. "This part of your life," Dr. Throng patiently explained to each new resident and then repeated once a week at the daily group meetings while Dr. Bledsoe nodded in a stentorian fashion behind her, "is just as real as the part where you have a career or a spouse or a child." Dr. Throng was a small woman with a blunt face and something Asiatic about her eyes. She had a quiet voice, spoke expressively with her hands and was universally beloved by all but the most hardened of the asocial aggressives of which Mary did not consider herself, although she had to admit she grew a little tired of straining forward to hear what Dr. Throng was saying.

"In the other world," Dr. Throng said, "you may get up in the morning and armor yourself in the clothes you wear for a day as a worker or a parent. You may put on a mask or practice a false emotional coloration, what in the animal world is called crypsis, as a means of defense against psychic barrage." She pressed her hands to her face and then her throat, made a fist and a fluttering motion to indicate intangible menace. "But here," Dr. Throng concluded every week, "you may get up in the morning and do whatever the experience of yourself encourages. Immerse yourself in yourself," she said. "And then tell us about it. That's all we ask of you."

The Have-Nots were, as Dr. Bledsoe put it, "more fully integrated into a private experience of the self." Which meant they were unstable to the point of grotesqueries, could not be trusted with their hygiene or personal responsibilities and made for unsavory company, to say the least. These residents, at least fifty of them by Mary's count, slept in separate dormitory style housing, at which a staff member was always on duty, and ate at a separate meal hour. They had their own individual and group therapy meetings and their activities around the facility's grounds were strictly controlled and constantly supervised. Mary and her compatriots, Donovan and August and Pete, sometimes caught sight of a group of Have-Nots being ushered from one building to another, a shambling line stooped with the enthralled torpor of the heavily medicated which progressed in moderate silence, emitting only the occasionally hoot or guttering cry. They were grim sight, unsettling. Enough to put one entirely out of the mood of one's day if Mary and her fellows had allowed it, which they did not. They were made of sterner stuff, Mary thought, and were also naturally the sort of people who gravitated toward the outer edge of their orbit. The sort of people who, if they were stars, would situate themselves so they could whirl right at the brink of the vast, black cosmos and peer in at the fissioning core of their galaxy with caustic skepticism.

"Barbarous," said Donovan, as he watched the line of the Have-Nots wind from the dining hall to the barn where they were to have a touch-therapy session with the goats. "In-transmutable," he muttered, pulling his mobile upper lip down over the wall of his long, yellow teeth.

Mary tended to agree, but August, who was tender-hearted and given to fits of despair over the abbreviation of such minor lives as ants and wasps, became quite inconsolable. He wandered into the river where he stood in an eddy and gazed upstream toward the point where the silver band of water jogged out of sight and higher to where it reappeared in a break in the trees as a sliver, a filament, a pure shining thread of the self that was rollicking over August's shins and wicking up his trouser legs. Mary could sympathize, up to a point. There was no doubt it was sad. There was something brittle about the air when the Have-Nots passed. Something crisp and rapacious like the thinnest edge of ice as it extends across the black void of a lake, though it was warm in the garden, practically balmy. Mary supposed it was betweeness she was feeling, a border she could sense and not see, or something like that. As soon as the Have-Nots were out of sight, she could not seem to bring herself to care. The garden was no help at all, festooned as it was with thrusting stands of blue iris, plump-headed daylilies, bobbing arm-lengths of lupine and speckled fox-glove clustered along their spears. Bees dipped and doddered everywhere. The birds were delirious. Mary chewed on a lime rind she fished from her glass and held it out to Pete who lifted the gin bottle from the coffee tin they were using as an ice bucket. From across the field, the ghost shouted, "Hi guys," and waved her arms above her head.

The ghost was a Have, but barely in Mary's estimation. In therapy sessions, when Dr. Throng asked them all to talk about why they were at the facility, August said, "I realized what I've been doing all these years is unforgivable, heinous."

Mary said, "I've swallowed a fly."

Donovan cycled through set answers, his favorite being, "I finally got around to reading Dostoevsky," and Pete refused to speak at all, expressing himself instead through a progressive blanching that left his face with the same gelid, near-translucency as an egg-white and his watery eyes blue as milk.

The ghost, who was maddeningly chipper, stated every day, "I am a rapid cycling manic-depressive with schizophrenic tendencies." She would look brightly around, beaming at each of them as if she were a kindergarten teacher leading the class in a sing-a-long. "Also, I have daddy issues," she would add, kicking up her feet and stretching her hands out into the circle as if she were leaning back against a line someone on the other end was holding taut.

The ghost was very pretty. She was younger than Mary, but not by so many years, and one could see from her demeanor, her relentless cheer, that she had previously been not so pretty.

In fact, she had most likely been plump and stodgy: the kind of girl Mary's grandmother would have sympathetically dismissed by saying, "Poor dumpling," and then, out of a sense of guilt, seated at her right hand during Mary's birthday party and made sure she got the slice of cake topped with the only unmaimed frosting rose. Somewhere in the ghost's young adulthood she had had a blossoming. Perhaps it was madness that became her, Mary didn't know, but in any event she had pleasant, regular features, oval white teeth, tiny ears behind which she could tuck her blonde hair with a truly enviable delicacy and stupendous knockers. In another ten years they would probably deflate entirely, but right then the ghost's breasts were suspended in their ripest moment, dropped fully into the form of themselves and depending from her prominent clavicle like two turgid drops of sap just about to slide from the lip of the wound down the smooth bark of their limb.

The ghost liked Pete and explained to them all that individuals with her diagnosis were frequently hyper-sexual beings as she stroked the inside of Pete's thigh and he froze, trembling with what Mary took to be nervous revulsion. The ghost also liked Mary and tended to follow her around the grounds and town proper making bright comments about the beauty of their surroundings, the simplicity of the native people, the dastardly nature of her father which she saw reflected in most items of the natural and manufactured world.

"My father was a real motherfucker," the ghost would say, fingering a hank of raw wool in the farmer's market. "One time, when I was thirteen, he purposefully opened the door on me going to the bathroom while he was giving the neighbors a tour of our new addition." She held her hand up to Mary's face and made her smell the musky lanolin odor that clung to her fingertips. "He died in '96. A car accident, entirely his fault, where a piece of rebar actually went straight through his heart. Isn't that funny, Mary?" the ghost asked, taking her arm at the elbow and pressing her breast against Mary's forearm. "Don't you think the guy selling the rhubarb is kind of cute?"

The ghost was also a mother, as was Mary although the ghost's children were quite a bit older. "Already pre-teens if you can believe it," said the ghost. Mary's child was very young, only a few months old. At the time her husband had flown with her to the facility so she could become a resident, it was still suckling from her breasts which were, even as she thought of it, pricking with squandered milk. This could have been quite an annoyance, but Mary found the longer she sat in the garden with Donovan and August and Pete, the more she held out her glass to be filled and felt inside her the fly—which had feather-light feet and shivered its wings as it walked inside her body so its edges felt like a snowflake tessellating permanently outward—the less she did think of her child (a boy, a son, they had named him Terry) and the smaller, firmer, more prepared her breasts became.

"These breasts are built for speed," she told Donovan, who looked at them appreciatively and laid a hand across her stomach as they lay in the grass. "These breasts are in training," she said.

"Oh, a little baby!" the ghost squealed when Dr. Bledsoe, in what was in Mary's opinion an almost criminally unprofessional breach of privacy, let it be known that she had recently had a child. "You must just be going crazy you miss him so much."

But that was it. Mary was not going crazy at all. It was just this fly, just its tickling progress around the environs of her gullet that was distracting her and making it so difficult to concentrate.

In her life outside of the facility, Mary had brought a lot of money to her marriage. And there's more where that came from, had been her father's catch phrase, though, it must be said, he employed it more often to indicate a reservoir of grit or anti-plutocratic *esprit-des-corps* than any measure of his substantial tangible wealth. This was not her husband Charlie's catch phrase. Charlie tended to look at the bitter side of things. If given a melon, whole and rare and thudding with summer, he would paw through its flesh looking for the seeds before he would take even one bite. Charlie had senatorial aspirations, though right now he was only a young partner in her father's firm. He had the broad, noble forehead and soft, wet mouth of a golden retriever and had wooed her in college by showing up at her dorm room unannounced with reservations to a Michelin-starred restaurant and box under his arm that contained a dress in just her size wrapped in pink tissue paper. It was a disgusting story, really; so boring. It was no wonder she didn't think of it now, Mary told August as he lit a cigarette for himself and then fished around in his pockets to find one for her.

She supposed it had been Charlie's idea that they have a child. They had not been married for very long and even before she was pregnant Mary had not worked. She preferred instead to drift around the two-hundred-year-old farmhouse her father had bought them as a wedding present picking up silver saltboxes from the credenza or a set of tortoiseshell-backed brushes from the upstairs powder room and carrying them out into the rambling back lawn where she left them to blacken in the grass. This was a kind of work, in her estimation, but, when she recalled it to herself, or to Pete who was a good listener, it sounded to Mary very much like a poor little rich girl story, which of course she had been, but was not what she meant at all. She was not telling a story, she explained to Pete who put his head in his hands and closed his eyes. Rather, she was just trying to live an empirical life, a life bolstered and actually improved upon by the fact that every part of it could be proven through physical evidence readily apprehended not only by the eyes, but by any other one of the senses possessed by a person of reasonable mental capacity. When she was in the house, Mary ran a piece of red chalk under the chair molding to mark her passage. When she was in the yard—more problematic, especially after a dry spell when the long grasses closed seamlessly behind her heels—she was forced to leave a scattering of objects, mobile monuments one could say, to stand in evidence of her hours. It was a project she had set for herself, she told Pete, speaking more hurriedly than she would have liked as she spotted the ghost approaching their table with a loaded plate. Something she had decided on in her teenage years, perhaps even as early as the dawn of her sexual awakening, as a measure against the obscurity of what she understood to be the fleeting score of her life.

Mary knew herself to be a determined woman, even a superlative woman, but the ongoing record of her life as she lived it was a demanding endeavor which began to take up more and more of her time. Charlie had determined her to be harebrained, charmingly scattered, a product of another age. But, when she abandoned the chalk and took to slicing the ball of her thumb and each of her fingertips with the fillet knife and leaving rambling ruby droplets through the conservatory and the parlor, up the front stairs into the bedroom, in ten tiny pools on the coverlet, down the backstairs and out into Charlie's vegetable patch, he suggested it might be time to procure for her a distraction.

"You must learn to be more careful with the knives," he had said, cupping her chin in his hand and turning her head from side to side as if seeking, and not finding, her eyes to gaze into. "Why don't we have a baby?" he had said and when she did not protest he pulled her onto his lap there on the stiff, horsehair stuffed sofa she had once thought made a sophisticated counterpoint to their ultra-modern globe lamps and slipped her nipple into his mouth.

∗∗∗

In group therapy, the ghost discussed her pregnancies. "I had my first baby when I was only fifteen. Can you believe it?" she said, shaking her head earnestly as if answering her own question. "And then I kept it! If you think that wasn't a monkey wrench in the works, well, you can think again, I guess."

It was a clear morning. A storm the night before had washed the air so clean breathing it was like spinning. It felt as if it were a late day in the week, but Mary didn't know which one nor, as calendars and other time marking devices were expressly discouraged, did she quite know how long she had been at the facility. If she consulted herself she might conclude it was around a month, perhaps a month and a half. The days seemed longer and hotter. The spent heads of the lilies crisped and withered on their stalks before the Have-Nots on garden duty got in there to pluck them green again, and the house wrens which had taken up residence under the eaves of her cottage were darting back and forth to their bosky nest with the cycling legs of insects clamped in their beaks rather than twigs and pine straw.

Therapy sessions were always held just before lunch. "When one's physical and mental acumen is at its height," said Dr. Bledsoe, and Mary could feel her hunger roiling up from her core like a spume of heated water. At about her sternum, the heat of her hunger stirred up the fly, which tended toward torpor, and she marked its progress as it buzzed around the pink vesicles of her lungs, pricked her heart with its sticky feet, descended to her liver where it unfurled its proboscis to eat. Mary considered that she had never felt stranger than she did at just that moment. In her previous, pre-fly life she would have felt compelled to commemorate this fact, but now she was content to sit, be still, to look inside. A wasp droned through the propped door and began to beat itself against the overhead light. Mary caught Donovan's eye and nodded up to it so they could watch together as the wasp experienced the self that was embroiled in this battle against the cut-glass shade.

The ghost was saying, "…frigid is the term for it, I think, or anyway the old-fashioned one, and my father really didn't have any other outlets because he was Catholic and took that very seriously, so instead he sublimated I supposed you would say, and turned all of our interactions into these really eroticized spaces where he'd be lifting me up to reach a light switch when I was little and he'd sort of hold my hand inside the shape of his and like breathe onto my cheek, or, you know, putting suntan lotion on my back, under the bathing suit straps and sort of lingering?"

Dr. Throng was taking notes, but Dr. Bledsoe, normally bent so fervently over his pad all Mary could see of him was his sleek part, was leaning back in his chair looking bored. He was watching the wasp too, Mary saw, tracking it with his eyes which, how had she never before noticed?, were a very intricate sort of hazel. He also had an intriguing mouth. It was thin and a little mean on top with a fat, tremulous, well-sucked looking lower lip posing an elegant counterpoint to his sharp, scythe-like chin. Mary tried to catch Donovan's eye again and call attention to her revelation about Dr. Bledsoe. Donovan was a self-confessed connoisseur of beauty. The more uninhabitable the better, he had said. Often, he could tell what she was thinking just by the expression on her face or the cant of her shoulders, but just now he seemed absorbed by the drama above him and didn't look at her. He pressed his fingers into his thighs as if playing a score on a piano, his knuckles whitening with pressure.

All around us the world is compressing itself like an accordion, Mary thought. Expressing itself of all its air so when it expands again it can make a tremendous, attention-calling racket.

The rat-box of the imagination, Mary thought.

***

It was when Mary was pregnant that she first became aware of the fly. Who knew when she had swallowed it, how long it had sat quiet in the unfamiliar puckers of her body before making itself known. So many things happened in a day, and she was so absorbed in marking their passage, it was sort of insulting to expect her to remember each little detail. The fly was probably very young, foolish and not used to complicated aerial navigation. Mary pictured its green iridescent carapace and the black hairs that bristled from its thorax. She envisioned its clear, articulate wings held at an angle from its body and thought she could feel when the fly moved blindly forward and when it stopped, scrubbing its face with its folded front legs as it tried to assimilate itself to this new life of darkness and pressure and clutching heat. When the fly came to Mary and passed through her lips as she slept or ate or walked down her sloping yard toward the creek, it would have felt like little more than half of a pill or a morsel of dry bread. It would have caused nothing more than a hitch in her breathing, an involuntary clutching swallow. For her, it was an instant, but think of the fly! It's whole world suddenly pink and convulsive. The wet terror it must have felt as it slid down, deeper down, away from the pleasures of the world and into an unremitting dark. No wonder it was shocked into stillness, stunned as surely as if it had been swatted from the air by her hand, and yet, however long it may have lain dormant, the fly lived and, feeling itself alive, somewhere in the middle months of her pregnancy it cocked its wings, buzzed them once, began to explore. In her second trimester Mary became suddenly and irrevocably aware of the fly's presence. Though she could not quite hear it buzz, she felt it travel.

"Morning sickness," said Charlie when she came to him and complained of this unprecedented sensation. At this stage, with her stomach beginning to assume the taut ovular shape so fetishized in the mother-to-be magazines Charlie kept buying and leaving about the house for her perusal, the only article of clothing Mary could tolerate against her skin was an old bikini she had bought for the sailing season some year in her teens when the white sails snapping crisp against the green-gold haze of the bay at dusk had seemed such an ordinary beauty she didn't even bother to observe it. The bikini had always been impractical, always gauche in an aggressive fashion that Mary thought suggested a deliberate deconstruction of both taste and money. It was made of gold lame with more closely woven silver palm trees situated over her nipples and pudenda. It had been quite expensive, she recalled, and even in its heyday had been an article of clothing meant to enhance rather than conceal nakedness. In her altered state, it must be said, the bathing suit was no longer doing any but the most nominal of duties to preserve her modesty. She swelled from it like dough rising emphatically out of its pan.

"You are essentially in the nude," said Charlie. In spite of their frequent coupling, he seemed to be more than usually bothered by this behavior and averted his eyes whenever she wandered into a room. "What if someone tries to deliver a package? Or knocks on the door to sell you a vitamin subscription?"

"They'll think I'm heading off for a swim," Mary said. She hardly even needed to hear Charlie anymore to know how to answer him. The baby twitched in its fishy way and the fly buzzed, as if in answer, scaled the ridged tubing of her esophagus and fizzed at her jaw line like a ruff made of ecstatic needles. She closed her eyes in order to better feel and the room receded from her—the slick of the waxed floorboards beneath her feet, the chill breeze wafting over her buttocks, the drone of Charlie's voice high and cyclic as a wasp's whine, all fell back from her as if she had shed the sensation like a cape or a gown, stepped out of the puddled fabric and onto a clean, smooth, empty stage.

Another time, Charlie came up behind her as she was picking hips off the rose trellis in the front garden and grabbed her by her own hips.

"You are not an animal," Charlie said, his breath puffing in hot, barely controlled bursts into her ear. He pulled her back and, though she could tell this wasn't his particular mood, her body did what she expected of it and she arced herself against him, rubbed. Charlie spun her around and shifted his grip to either side of her collarbone. "You are not going to shit this baby out in a ditch," he said. His eyes were dilated, the pupils looking sweetly baffled if one ignored the expression on the rest of his face. He shook her and dug his thumbs in under her clavicle. "You're not going to leave it squalling and wander off leaking a trail of blood. You are a woman," he shook her, "a wife," he shook her. "Put some clothes on; put your tongue back in your mouth. Stop being such a cunt," Charlie said. He thrust her away as if she were the one who had infringed on his space and strode back into the house.

For Charlie, this was quite a display. Mary lost her balance— so topsy, so weeble-wobble in those final weeks. She caught herself on the rose trellis with some difficulty and at the expense of several crushed blooms and a row of punctures in her palm where the thorns dug in. The next morning, as she slipped the bikini strings over her head and fingered a new tear in the over-stretched fabric, she noticed a pair of bruises like iridescent false eyes stamped on either side of her chest where Charlie's thumbs had pressed. Still, she could not find it in herself to feel outrage or concern. Charlie slunk around the house like a dog that has peed again on the rug and even at the time, with the swell of the baby and the drone of the fly forming a barrier between them, she had felt supremely distanced from the whole event. She had watched as her hand swanned across the impossible space between them and stroked Charlie between the eyes. She had even, had she not?, slipped two of her fingers between his lips to feel the broad heat of his tongue.

No, she had not done those things, but it didn't matter. She could have and in the night she watched Charlie sleep and thought nothing of him. She pressed her thumbs against his eyelids and felt his eyes twitch and roll beneath her pressure. She concluded he was like the anatomical model her father had given her when she was eight. A visible man whose parts were all painted realistic colors and inserted so that their tubes and valves lined up in the correct fashion, but who was nevertheless just plastic in temporary stasis. An object at the mercy of any passing creature's whim to bat him about or open him up and rearrange. Charlie's problem was that he was uninhabited, Mary thought. He could never say that he was being, only that he had been. He had no proof, Mary thought and gently peeled back his eyelids so she could see the blank crescent of his eyes as they rolled back and forth in his head.

And then the baby came.

She remembered a time of panting, of constriction. In reality, this was very much like squatting over some weed-rank ditch and slicking a path with her blood, but with more people present, a greater preponderance of cartoon patterning in the nurse's scrubs and peach tones in the purportedly soothing color scheme of her private labor room. Charlie was there saying something very close to her ear. There was a sharp pop, like the sensation she always supposed the television in her father's study felt as its picture dwindled into a white-hot point, and Charlie was gone. Something in the room made a high, gasping wail, and the fly continued to sip at her juices, wholly unconcerned.

That was really the clincher. She didn't understand why no one else could understand her position. The baby, though intricate in its parts, was not absorbing. Rather, it absorbed and seemed perfectly content to hang at her breast grunting and rooting around with its puckered, puffy lips. The fly, on the other hand, was unique and her relationship with it required a sort of undivided attention to the experience she could not afford if she were to continue with her extant duties of the home. Indeed, in what Mary considered the *coup d'etat* of her thus far single-minded life, she had totally abandoned her record making in favor of delving more deeply into the daily intricacies of the fly's behavior. This necessitated that she spend a great deal of time in a prone position, either in the slender guest bed Charlie had moved her into for what he termed her recovery, or on the horse-hair sofa with her feet propped on the uncomfortably baroque armrest. There she would lie with her eyes closed and every part of her anatomy slowed to its most somnambulant measure. It might have seemed like sleep, Mary conceded, or even a sort of trance state, but really this was an expression of deep concentration. Of an inward gaze so finely tuned it skipped over mere meditation and became a sort of transcendence wherein she and the small, improbable life that was going on inside her merged and were one. It was inspiring. She herself was inspired. Meanwhile, Charlie spent a great deal of time pacing around the house with the baby in one arm and the phone propped between his chin and shoulder. That was his choice. She supposed he could not help his limitations.

"I am finally getting to the work of my life," Mary said, and Charlie, whacking the baby on the back with one tanned hand as it jiggled and coughed said, "I've heard of a really great place, up north, in the mountains, for a rest. What do you think?"

The ghost's father was, apparently, quite a bad man. He was the worst kind of man who would do a thing in such a way so that later he could convincingly deny it. It was probably all in her head: the way his hand had lingered, the way his breath had puffed. But then again, by her own confession, the ghost had been a clumsy girl, always in harm's way. And wasn't she constantly arriving in such a fashion as to suggest her willingness? "I'm up for anything," the ghost had often said in her, Mary's, hearing. It was practically a mantra.

Oh, this was all so exhausting. All Mary had wanted was to be a pretty girl walking through a parking lot. When she walked on the asphalt she would hear the clickety-clack of her little black heels stuffed full of her little white feet. When she stepped up onto the median she would feel the faintest tear as she punctured perfectly round holes in the sod. A pretty girl who had two or three boys to talk to and long hair she could flip over one shoulder and a car waiting at the corner that would pick her up and whisk her away, silent behind the passenger glass, bound for an unknown fate.

The ghost said, "In a weird way, I think I can't forgive him because he never did it. I mean not all the way. If he had it's like it would have confirmed something, you know? But as it is I feel like I'm in a small room with a lot of other people, and the air conditioning's broken or something, and maybe somebody farted but maybe they didn't. Do you know what I mean? Like maybe I can smell somebody's fart but it's just the hint or whisper of a fart and I'm sniffing and sniffing to tell whether I can smell it or not and suddenly I realized that this is all I'm doing anymore. Sniffing for someone's fart." The ghost sniffed rich and deep through flared nostrils to demonstrate for them and turned to Dr. Bledsoe with her hands folded in her lap. Mary resisted the urge to sniff with her, an almost overwhelming impetus to mimicry. Mental contagion, she thought. The last thing she needed was someone else's flotsam cluttering up her mind.

"I think that's all I have to say," the ghost said, beaming, and the woman sitting next to her put her hand on the ghost's arm in a universal gesture of empathy. Mary rolled her eyes.

"Fine, that's fine. Very good," said Dr. Bledsoe. He slipped the tip of his pen from between his mismatched lips and used it to point across the circle to Mary. "Mrs. Madrill, I believe you're the only one left?"

Well, what could he have expected? By this point, Mary felt as if her voice was sliding down a pair of well-worn tracks entirely independent of will or volition. Her voice was like a mine cart, propelled by gravity, which might reasonably be trusted to guide its own way into the interior darkness of the earth. She could leave it alone and come back later to see what she had said.

"I am here because I swallowed a fly," Mary said. She folded her own hands primly in her lap and used the rest of her allotted twenty minutes to follow the progress of the wasp which beat herself silly against the unheeding light and finally collapsed to the floor in a tightly curled ball of exhaustion and hurt. The fly buzzed at around the level of her small intestine in either alarm or sympathy. Dr. Bledsoe sucked his pen. Between them, Mary considered, something else was being said.

Later that evening, Mary was in the garden. Startlingly, she was alone.

Alone the noise the river made was more apparent than when she was engrossed with a conversation or a companionable listening silence. In fact, Mary thought as she tipped the last drops of her gin onto the petals of a delphinium, closed up for the night, and poured herself some more from the bottle, the river was positively raucous. It sounded as if it were in the middle of a frivolous, but absorbing discussion. As if it were actually many rivers all talking at once. Mary took a turn around the garden. She held her cup at an elegant angle from her body, her arm outstretched like the long, white, elegant neck of a crane and her hand just as cruel and fast as its head which was, after all, mostly beak. She was really quite drunk, that old veil down over her eyes so the garden seemed to swim to meet her focus in particular parts which were difficult to anticipate. Here was a coiled vine descending from the trellis; here a paper plate smeared across its face with a streak of mustard. Mary found herself in amongst the irises whose gentian blooms were all stiffly furled. "Come open," someone said in a thick, gargling voice and Mary saw it was her own fingers that were sliding over the tops of the plants but could seem to get no purchase.

Well, how absurd. Mary was not above laughing at herself. She had once had a conversation with her father about that very subject in which he had said she was a fine girl. "Fine as horses," he had said, running his finger in an arc around the corners of her mouth, but she was altogether too dramatic.

"You'll find the earth is quite resentful," her father had said to her. They had been somewhere. A forest of some sort. The memory was insubstantial, but Mary seemed to see her father sitting on a log, the rotted wood crumbling beneath him as he shifted his weight. His hands were dangling between his knees and he was wearing a butter yellow shirt, something with a collar. His hair was mussed. For the life of her, Mary could not think what she and her father might have been doing out in the woods, but she had been a biddable child, likely to follow anyone anywhere given only the slightest encouragement. Probably she hadn't even been invited. That would have been just like her, Mary thought and snorted.

She had come to the lone spruce again, was coming back around to the trellis and picnic table. The route was getting easier and easier. Her feet seemed so light and independent it was as if she were prancing about the garden like a pony. A white pony, like Bert, with a black clown mask like Bert had hiding her eyes. Mary tossed her mane and picked up her pony feet.

"The earth's already got two strikes against every living thing," her father said. There was something wrong with one of his eyes. Or maybe it was the way he was looking at her with it. His finger went around and around her mouth which was wet and sticky with some sort of berry or punch as children's mouths often are. There was something so wrong with one of her father's eyes! Oh, she felt sorry for him and also as if she had neglected something, an action she was supposed to perform or a certain knowledge she was supposed to have committed to memory. Mary shook her head, but could not clear it. It appeared the fly had flown up from her gullet and was fidgeting now behind her eyes. This was neither pleasant nor exactly unmenacing, but, Mary supposed, the fly was evolving as all things evolve. Trying things out. Seeing what stuck.

"It's better just to stay out of sight," her father said, "Escape notice. Do you know what I mean?"

Mary couldn't remember if she knew what her father meant or not, but all this was in the past, the enormous past, and now she was going around and around the garden, greeting again each thing that swum up at her with wholly honest surprise and delight. "I am here as much as I am," Mary told the fly and found, as she had worried she eventually might, that she was standing in the middle of the river, balanced atop a sandy hummock with river water curling against her shins and tugging at her ankles.

It wasn't so bad. The river was cold, a deep aching cold that could only come from some very high place like the top of a mountain. Or outer space, Mary briefly considered, but no, this was no time for hubris. The river was cold because it came from the mountain where everything was always very cold. Even the little birds and animals, the rabbits with their incendiary eyes, were so cold their flesh shrank inside their feathers or fur until they were much much smaller than they appeared to be. The river came down from the mountain and, as it came, it had a long conversationwith itself, and now here was Mary, right in the middle of it all. The fly moved higher in her head, buzzing up and down just below the crown of her skull. It was surely still a very small fly, Mary thought, to be able to travel about so freely, but it didn't feel small and now, as it picked its way across the folds of her brain, it was also starting to feel quite demanding. The best thing to do might be to ignore it. Give it a taste of its own medicine. She dug her toes under the smooth rocks and coarse sand of the riverbed. The moon was full and high and in its light her skin and the river water took on the same sheen. It was easier said than done. "What do you want?" Mary said to the fly, but she got no answer. Out of the corner of her eye, she caught the quick flurry of something that has been startled into motion and then freezes again, hoping not to be seen.

Mary stood in the middle of the river and looked. She knew where it was, right there under the white bridge that crossed the river just beyond the old mill house. Right there, in the shadow where the crisp white pylon was cut by the dark water. But it was not there. There was nothing there but the pylon, the sandy bank, the river. Still. Mary was certain. It was suffering her gaze. It was breathing in apprehension. It was poised to rush—which way? toward her? poised to spring? It was waiting for her next move which would have to be so deliberate, her most carefully balanced move to date. What would it be? This test, which she had always anticipated, had come upon her so suddenly, when she was so preoccupied with other considerations. On paper, it might appear that Mary was in the worst possible state to accept such a challenge, but, she thought, perhaps after all this was the only state in which such challenges could be proffered. Her dress fluttered forward between her legs, caught in the breeze of the river. It was important to articulate herself as both predator and prey; it was important to indicate the hard kernel of self that had never before been breached. Mary mustered all her resources. The fly buzzed furiously, each bristle erect. There was nothing there; she was sure. "Dr. Bledsoe?" she said and flung out her hand.

Fifteen years later, Mary sat in a wicker chair looking down the long slope of her yard to the creek where her children were playing. It was late summer, the land booming at the height of its hollow greenness. Some time earlier, Mary had slipped off her shoes and she wiggled her toes in the grass and considered the experience, as she always did, less satisfactory than the idea of the experience which conveniently elided the fact of insect life, now making itself known by crawling across her feet with the most unpleasant lack of surprise. As if every day great, pale mountains came out of the sky to sit heavily on their fertile fields. As if there was no longer anything under the sun that could elicit the awe of a grasshopper.

An ant crossed Mary's toenail and she flicked her foot so briskly it flew off and landed what must have seemed an unfathomable distance away in the grass next to the coffee tin Terry had filled with ice for her. Mary sipped her drink. Her children were singing some sort of a song together. It didn't seem as if Terry knew the words, but Irma, who was patient and stolid, was repeating the song phrase by phrase so he could mimic her. Mary couldn't see the children, but heard them splashing and singing and every now and then caught a glimpse of their bodies as they crossed before a break in the trees.

Probably they were swimming naked again. It seemed likely from both her prior knowledge of their proclivities and the amount of skin she saw flashing in between the weighty limbs of the cottonwood and river birch. This bothered Charlie to no end, particularly now that Irma was older and Terry, a long, bronze, ill-tempered boy, had acquired all the physical heraldry of a man.

Mary supposed it should bother her, too. After all, she was there with them, day after day, season after season. If someone was tasked with instilling in the children an appropriate wrath toward their bodies, it was most likely to be her, their mother, who had rolled them from nits to full, pearly skeletons in the tumbler of her womb, but Mary could not bring herself to do so. "Let them wallow in it. For awhile more," Mary said to no one. There was no one there. Not even a garden, which was tucked up around the skirts of the house in neatly demarcated beds Charlie paid a gardening service to weed and prune and turn. Around Mary was nothing but the swale of clipped grasses and the sky which seemed to come closer and closer every year. The tree line started on her side of the creek and extended beyond it all the way to the highway which was barely visible, a shining scar slashed along the flank of the nearest foothill, and Mary wasn't sure if the droning she was hearing was from the distant cars or a chant of the insects or some other kind of effect originating from inside her own ears and radiating out.

Mary finished her drink and set it on the wide, wooden arm of the chair. She closed her eyes and watched the hot pattern the sun made against her eyelids. Mary was forty-five. For the past eight years, since Irma's birth, the fly had been a leaden pea within her chest, utterly still. She supposed this meant it had finally acceded to the natural order of things, the body finally triumphing over the will; yet, the fly didn't feel dead to her. It felt as if it were in hibernation. It felt acquiescent. Regardless, she supposed she no longer needed the measures she and Charlie had implemented to keep the fly in check when it became too frivolous with its use of her resources, but they were a habit, part of a routine toward which she felt some responsibility. She went on.

Often, Mary was resting. This was the word they all used around the house. She didn't know what her children might say of her when they were outside of the house, and she didn't consider it her business. Outside the house, her children wore pants and shoes. They opened their fat pretty mouths and out spilled the most banal and complicated things, like hurky monkeys which clapped their cymbals to no discernable rhythm. Mary knew this was true, though she had hardly ever witnessed it. She was not so far gone, she considered, pouring herself another drink, that she did not know the ways in which the world ordered itself. For example, she could stand up right now and walk down the slope after which she could reasonably expect herself to arrive at the creek. There she could tell her children, who would be arcing from the water like otters or some other creature that makes full utility of its skin, to gather up the garments they have left in a heap on the bank and clothe themselves, each arm through an arm hole, each leg through the hole that has been sewn to fit a leg. It was even likely that the children would do so—they were fond of her in a distant, jovial way—but to what purpose? This was something Mary often asked herself. To what purpose was the earth?

The ghost arrived from somewhere in the direction of the driveway and sat in the grass at Mary's side. "Hello," the ghost said, and when Mary didn't respond she pulled a blade of grass from the ground and made a little whistle of it which she blew with grating regularity as she looked around her. Clearly, Mary had forgotten something. She felt as if she had just embarked on a long trip only to recall some important piece of identification which might be in her wallet or might be tucked in the pocket of her winter coat, hung tidily in the hall closet. Either way, to look would set something resolutely in motion, would define, in any contingency, a certain lack. Mary kept her eyes resolutely forward.

The last time Mary had seen the ghost was her last morning at the facility on which she had awoken on the floor of her cottage amidst a heap of bedding and meditation pillows. Impelled by some unfathomed instinct, she had immediately risen and walked, still shoeless, still in her damp dress, toward the dining hall where she discovered something had occurred in her absence. There had been a fire, a grievous one. It had swept through the floors of the Have-Nots' dormitory in the last hours of the night, perhaps bursting into its first blue spark even as she, Mary, was winding her way back from the garden. There were many casualties. Though the fire was now out, as Mary stumbled up behind Donovan and August and Pete who were standing in a loose circle, turned partially away from the scene but still craning to look, she could see the smolder of the building rising hot against the sky. There was a smell. There was a high buzzing whine that seemed to be spilling out of many people's mouths at once. A woman in a purple nightdress sat on one of the railroad ties that defined the parking lot and rubbed her singed hair off her head in clumps. A fireman knelt in the damp gravel and tugged something straight beneath a sheet. Mary did not see Dr. Bledsoe, though she looked for him, but she did see the ghost who was standing in the shade of an apple tree, her hands clasped between her breasts as if holding some small, imprisoned creature. The ghost's mouth was slack and heavy. She was watching, avariciously, Mary thought, as the fireman turned the waning flow of their hoses on this sooty pile, on that steaming beam, in a final wavering line around the base of the gutted building, before cranking off the water and coiling the hoses for storage.

"Look at that," Mary said, but Donovan and August and Pete all continued to look at whatever detail of the scene had originally caught their attention. There was a brown clog lying on its side next to a puddle of greasy water. There was a sunny yellow curtain, entirely intact, snapping through the blackened frame of a window. The boys were like pillars of salt, struck into crumbling particularity, and they did not acknowledge her. When she put her hand on August's arm she felt him vibrating beneath her touch like something that had been wound very tightly and then kept from moving. Dr. Throng, wearing jeans and an unflattering orange silk pajama top, was running back and forth along the path between the dormitory and the dining hall talking on her cell phone. The hand not holding the phone was clenched perfectly still at her side. Donovan said, "The fools, the idiots," but he was not talking to her and, when she followed the line of his gaze, he seemed to be staring at the goat barn, through the windows of which the heads of the four nannies could be seen racketing about, the animals struck into a hereditary terror by the smell of the charred wood. There were five sheets covering uneven shapes laid before the building. Pete was flushed and kept sticking his fingers into his mouth as if perhaps he had burned them. There was a yellow warbler which perched briefly on a car antenna and then sprung away, warbling. There was something on the ground, a lump of something on the ground which was black and maroon and seemed to leak. There was the river, unperturbed, winking in and out of sight between the line of ambulances and fire trucks.

Later that day, Charlie, who had caught an inconvenient flight and hired a driver at the airport, came to pick her up. All of the resident's emergency contacts had been called. Cars were parked in untidy clusters before all the buildings and men and women in an array of hastily contrived outfits were leading their parents, or spouses, or grown, unreliable children around by the wrists, or standing with their hands cupped around their mouths, shouting names into the calamitous air. Charlie looked tired, but also somehow fresh. He was doing something different with his hair, wearing it longer over his forehead which lessened the severity of his mournful eyes. The car parked on the white bridge, as close as it could get to the crowded scene, and Charlie and the driver carried her bags from her cottage, all the way around the barn and greenhouse, through the muddy sward surrounding the dining hall and extant dormitory and set them at her feet beside the car.

The driver was a tall man with crisp, tightly curled hair. He was distracted by the scene and stood for a minute on the bridge, shaking his head and whistling silently between his teeth as he took it in. Mary thought how strange it was that this was likely all she would ever know of the driver: his haircut and his habits of surprise. It didn't seem enough, though she supposed what else was there? Charlie too stood looking over the side of the bridge, though he kept away from the railing as if he feared anything he touched would wipe off on his clothes. No one seemed to notice her. She brushed her hands against her dress and noticed for the first time that it was the plum dress, one of her favorites, very beguiling in the way it plunged at the neck and flowed at the thigh. She felt a little dizzy.

Charlie looks like a flower blooming just before the frost, Mary thought and then she was annoyed with herself for having made such a topical analogy. Still, once thought the image stuck. Bloom before doom, Bloom before doom, she thought with an irritating shrillness. She was probably coming undone. It could be excused. After all, there had been a tragedy. Mary considered that she needed a drink and, as she waited for the driver and Charlie to finish loading her bags, found that this was exactly the sort of car in which drinks were provided. There were even plastic cocktail stirrers in an array of jewel-tone colors; little plastic swords and others that were topped with little plastic daisies. The fly came up to the very top of her throat and into her mouth where it tapped against the backs of her teeth, but would not or could not exit. Mary stirred her drink with an emerald sword and watched the landscape slide away around her. The car was fast and smooth and seemed to travel with a fierce possessiveness. From where she sat,

Mary could see the back of the driver's black head over the top of Charlie's blond one.

Everything was in such opposition it was hard to feel like a whole person. Black head, blond head. Mountain, river. Even when Mary closed her eyes, there was the fly, scrubbing its face at the back of her tongue, confused, battered. Even with her eyes closed, she knew when the world around her lurched into motion—the moment when it gathered itself into hallucinatory precision and then slipped away.

Mary had been so preoccupied with the car and the drink and the sharp emerald sword which she now used to prick her finger, that she had taken no last look behind her, had said goodbye to no one. She had just left. Swallowed up like nothing other than herself standing in her own body on the great, hot tongue of a giant. So this was how it had gone, Mary thought and sucked the swelling drop of blood from off her finger. It tasted like pine, but probably she had slopped some gin on her finger. That was probably the only explanation.

"You were in no real danger?" Charlie said, leaning forward and putting a hand on her knee. "You're all still in one piece?"

Charlie's hand was warm and sloppy and large. It enveloped her knee which, she realized, was looking a little rackety. She still wasn't wearing any shoes and her feet against the impeccable floor mats looked like little animals turned out of their skins.

"I'm pretty tired," Mary said to her husband. She felt she was admitting to something else entirely. She felt the release of confession.

"I bet," Charlie said, walloping her knee in a friendly gesture. He lurched across the space between them and settled next to her, tucked her under his arm so her head rested in his armpit where she could smell his thin, clean cologne. "I hope none of those ones were anyone you knew," Charlie said, looking out the other window, his hand pressed over Mary's ear so his voice came to her as if through the chambers of a shell.

"No," Mary said. "I didn't know anyone there." It was true, she thought. Just not at the time.

After all that, it was startling to say the least to have the ghost turn up. Out of the clear blue, as it were, though actually the sky was a different color than blue. It was white and, underneath, violet. It was like the white powder that covers the skin of an unripe plum. Mary thought she handled her surprise admirably. She took a sip of her drink and looked at the ghost only out of the corner of her eye.

"Don't you remember me?" the ghost said, pouting and shifting her weight so she could tuck her legs beneath her and bring herself up closer to Mary's eye-line. "Oh, I know you do, silly. It's me? Remember? It hasn't been that long."

Mary thought she might scream, out of irritation, surely, but it turned out to be a burp which rose from her stomach to the top of her throat and then subsided without finding expression. It had been such a non-descript day, so expected. Mary noticed the ghost's shadow huddled around her knees with the same watery meagerness as Mary's own. The sun was almost directly overhead. It beat along Mary's part and made her hair feel hot and crisp. I should wear a hat, Mary thought, and noticed, with some satisfaction, that her prediction about the ghost's breasts had been correct. The ghost wore a marmalade tank top and a pair of cropped linen trousers. There were deep lines creasing her forehead and her lips were seamed and puckered, impressed with an uneasy orange lipstick. Her ears were still tiny, however; delicate as twin halves of a pistachio shell. Her hair was still bright and blond.

"Would you like a drink?" Mary said at last. She groped around her feet for the bottle, keeping her eyes fixed on the tree line though the children had stopped singing, stopped splashing, seemed preoccupied with some other, quieter, play. She could find the bottle nowhere. She groped and groped, but all she kept touching was her own ankle. Anyway. It didn't matter.

"That's alright," said the ghost, waving her hands at Mary as if shooing her away. "I stopped a while ago. Years ago, it would be now. I had an infection, supposed to be nothing serious, but then it was something else and then something else until finally it was just easier to never drink a drop again, and you know me, bull by the horns." The ghost laughed and clutched Mary's forearm where it lay against the chair's wooden arm, had lain all this time perfectly inert and lax like a dead snake. The ghost's hands were dry. She scratched at Mary's skin with her nails in a friendly fashion and then folded her hands back in her lap.

"Well," said Mary, vaguely. The children were coming up the hill. Terry came first and Irma following him with all of their clothes rolled into a bundle which she pressed to her chest. Terry had a blue towel slung around his neck. They looked so alike, her children, though Terry of course was taller and there were other obvious differences. They both had oval faces and even features, straight dark brows, definitive noses which came to a fragile crest between their eyes. They were tanned all over as if they had been cut with one swoop of the scissors and not pieced together in so many scraps as other people's children must seem to be. Terry rubbed his hair with the towel and waved.

"And how have you been otherwise?" Mary said to the ghost who had canted her hand over her eyes like a visor and was peering down the hill. Mary took a sip of the dregs of her drink. The missing bottle was bothering her somewhat and she moved her foot, hoping she would strike against it with her heel. It was supposed to be around here somewhere; everything was supposed to be around here somewhere, but Mary knew it was not. It had gone. It was disappeared.

The ghost laughed, a high, twittering laugh, and grabbed Mary's forearm as if for ballast. Mary thought of things she had not thought of in years. The garden, the river. The sound of the trees high on the mountain as they rubbed against each other. "Well, I died, of course," said the ghost, still giggling. "You're so funny, Mary. But let's see, other than that…" The ghost tapped her teeth as she thought, a gesture Mary had forgotten. Irma dropped Terry's sandals and he waited for her as she picked them up, readjusted her bundles. He really was a nice brother, testing her mostly in reasonable ways. Terry's hair was very long. He claimed to have never once cut it, though Mary thought this could not be right. Still, seeing it now clinging darkly to his shoulders and down his back, it was possible to believe the very tips of his hair were the same thin, silky strands he had as a baby. The alien hair he already had when he was born.

"Well, I got married and then later on I got married again," the ghost said, nudging her. "Get it? Anyway, we bought a house and then my second husband was kind of an animal nut so we had a lot of weird ones. Different kinds of lizards and for a couple of years this horse named Bobo that my husband would just let come into the house. I swear, he walked around in there like a dog or something. Putting his nose on the countertops, everything!" The ghost was delighted by this, delighted to tell it. Mary imagined a horse wandering glumly through some kind of split-level. She imagined the imprint his hooves would make on the carpeting. "And my kids grew up, of course," the ghost said, still watching Terry and Irma as they resumed their journey. "You remember them, right? I talked about them all the time."

"Of course," Mary said. She remembered very little, she realized. She remembered a sound someone made that she found annoying, some habitual sound of their body, but not what it was or who it came out of. Most of the things she thought of now hadn't happened yet, or, like the horse, hadn't happened to her. "A boy and a girl, wasn't it?" Mary said.

"No!" said the ghost, rocking back on her heels, preparing to stand. "Oh, Mary, I see you haven't lost your sense of humor. I always did so admire your perspective. But you remember, two girls, Beverly and Dumma. Dumma was this passing fancy I had, I was only eighteen when she was born after all, but later I really came to regret it. Such an ugly, frumpy name and, chicken before the egg I suppose, she turned out to be a kind of ugly, frumpy girl. Oh, and with an ugly spirit too, like her father, not a lot of fun to be around, but what can you do? Your child will always be the strangest of the strangers in your life, don't you think?" The ghost had risen and backed out of Mary's sightline. She was somewhere behind her, the voice drifting away toward the house as if the ghost were wandering toward the nearest bed of dispirited monkey-grass wilting in its solitary clumps. Irma ran forward the last few yards. She flung her bundle of clothes at Mary's feet and collapsed on top of them giggling. Her buttocks were so brown they seemed more like the haunches of an animal downed with a light, white fur.

"No," said Mary, "that's not what I think at all." But of course it was. It was just exactly what she thought.

"What?" Terry said. He sat in the grass and stretched his legs out in front of him. Mary could see the bottoms of his tough feet, the hard, yellow calluses at the ball of his foot and his heel. He laid the blue towel across his lap with an incidental air that Mary thought was quite insolent. "What did you say?" her child asked.

When Irma was born, the fly had settled in her midsection, only sporadically agitated into fitful buzzing as if it had landed on its back and was trying to right itself, and finally stilled completely. Mary had not expected this. After so many years, she assumed the vagaries of the fly to be a condition of her body—something to be attended to like her moles, which often now clustered into pre-malignant constellations, but nothing to get too keyed up about. One must live, after all. One must travel around and pick things up and put them down again.

However, Irma herself had been something of a surprise. There was a question as to her provenance. In those days, with the fly to anchor her and her time in the facility a matter of polite public secret, Mary was quite the dish. When she arrived on the scene, she felt the scene shift to accommodate her. She had beau-tiful teeth, small and sharp. She had really terrific calves and long, languid thighs which she enjoyed stroking as one would a disqui-eted child during lulls in the conversation. They had joined a party of Charlie's peers on a yacht owned by one of the firm's senior partners. There had been champagne and gin and shrimp curled atop tiny triangles of toast. There had been a dessert centerpiece, some kind of layered pudding studded with red and orange dahl-ias which seemed to leap into the air and burst like a simulacrum of fireworks which was exactly the image they were intended to present. Mary admired the dessert's dedication to artifice. How precisely the dahlia became a firework at its apex and would, as the petals withered and fell, resemble as well the firework at its descent. How cleverly the pallid surface of the pudding, which shuddered with each thud of the beating engine as they motored out of the harbor, resembled in both fact and theory the shudder-ing surface of the ocean currently surrounding them with an air of preoccupied silence.

It was dusk. The sun was splashing outlandish colors across the horizon. There was a band, a strange combo of drum, gui-tar and trumpet, playing softly on the aft deck, an open bar do-ing swift business on the fore and an exclusive company invited aboard—only two other couples, not counting the owner and his wife, whose names were Chris and Kris and Donald and Pet. Mary had never met them before. They were new, the men up-and-comers, the women having something to do with real estate, or, in Pet's case, the trauma room at the hospital. Appropriately, Pet had a scrubbed look about her as if her face had been washed so many times all her features had been pushed away from one another. Her eyebrows were charming, dark and sparse. Chris and Kris, on the other hand, were horribly unremarkable. They had an indeterminate number of children. Many children, Mary gathered and she imagined the weird dislocation the children must feel at the fact of their parents' names. How unnatural to know at such a young age that there were really no choices in the world, that somewhere a man or a woman named Chris was carving a space into which one would fit. It was oppressive, obscene. Kris was wearing a very pretty claret dress, entirely out of season, and Chris had a round head, round eyes, a round mouth pursed like a rectum. Mary took an instant dislike to them both.

The yacht was captained and crewed by a company of sailors who wore tidy, anachronistic uniforms with gold braid at the shoulders and widely cuffed pants, but it was owned by the senior partner in Charlie's firm who had been a friend of the family since Mary was just a very little girl. He had been a friend of her father's and had come to her childhood house with a different wife and sat out on the patio with her father and the other men smoking and accepting brown drinks in sturdy tumblers. His name was Walter Smit, though he had always admonished her to call him Wally. Once, when she was about six, Wally had picked her up and put her on the top shelf of the closet amongst the hats and gloves. He had shut the door on her in there and Mary had sat quietly, kicking her legs in the total, uncomplicated dark. It had been wonderful. Eyes open or eyes shut, it made no difference. Mary considered that something important was being shown to her: a mystery of adulthood, a way to still the ticking clock of her mind. Then, Wally opened the door and she saw it was all meant to be a joke. He lifted her down, his hands pinching under her armpits, and guffawed. He ruffled her hair.

She had never forgiven him, not even at her father's funeral where he seemed genuinely disturbed, as she had been, by the funeral home's choice of floral display: waxy bursts of frangipani interwoven with fans of pink gladioli. There was a terrible smell of shoe polish in the room where the service had been held. Several people, including Mary herself, were quite drunk and an elderly aunt from an unknown branch of the family had arrived with an entourage of small black dogs from which she could not be persuaded to part. The dogs sat on the pew beside her, three of them, looking upright and insincere. Wally sat in the pew directly behind Mary and she felt he had looked at her far too much during the service. She had felt the unspoken pressure of his gaze and, sensitive as she knew herself to be to outside influence, knew her experience had been altered by it. Was there nothing, then, that could be savored? Was there no life that could be lived outside the bidden realm? Mary thought she might tilt her head back and say to Wally, from the corner of her mouth, "I don't remember you at all, you know," but she did not and then the time for it had passed. Then more than a few years had passed, and here she was on Wally's boat.

"It *is* a lot of children," Pet was saying to Kris. They were on the foredeck near the bar. The crew maneuvered the boat out of the mouth of the bay and into open water and cut the engine. Over the creak of the booms and the whipping of ropes and sails, the band could be heard blatting and thumping, some one of the men energetically calling out encouragement. Mary had no expectations of this moment. She watched Charlie as he dipped his head toward Wally's wife, Dina, who was unusually petite, almost pint-sized, and had lurid violet nails which she was using to shred the napkin wrapped around her drink. A nervous woman, Mary thought, a woman who is afraid of her body. Mary let the moment wash around her and then the next and the next after that. She inclined against the railing and watched the shoreline pass, ragged with houses and shore-grass, concrete pylons and wading birds.

"There is a special kind of bandage," Pet was saying, "a very small kind of bandage which we keep in stock." Kris was pressing her hand against the tanned expanse of her cleavage. The conversation had turned on her. Mary imagined a long gallery full of inordinately small beds. Inside each was a child wrapped in specially stocked bandages which had been ordered long before the child's accident or wasting illness, imagined for them when each child was whole and rosy and in control of all its parts. There was something so honest about a hospital, Mary thought. Planning for the future. She wished she was standing a little closer to Pet so she could tell her as much. She seemed the sort of woman who felt an intimacy with the macabre, a woman who understood the danger of palliative thinking, but she and Kris appeared to be getting along like a house on fire. Charlie took Dina by the elbow and led her into a short, jogging waltz. Chris clapped his fleshy hands together as if they were two hunks of roasted meat he had found at the end of the spit and Donald was nowhere to be seen. Mary felt integral to the scene in an odd way, like a caryatid, but a kind of slouching one. One who resented the weight of the pediment but considered it déclassé to rail against oppression or hoard golden apples, flee before the onslaught of the gods or whatever other sort of the thing a woman was expected to do in myth and architecture.

When Wally appeared at her side and laid a hand on her hip, Mary was not surprised. In the intervening years he had grown lean and sinewy, his features starkly disassociated from one another so the nose and the mouth, the ears and the eyes seemed to have only a passing relationship. He was poised in a golden moment in his life, his age upon him but not yet within him, his body comfortable in solitude. "Planning for the future," she told him, instead, and he said, "You've become something else. Not a woman. Some other thing. How exactly did that happen?"

From there, it was short order.

She and Wally came together in a sort of a stateroom in the belly of the yacht. They were under the waterline, the water sometimes splashing to the halfway mark of the porthole windows set high on the curved hull where it slopped and foamed in just the way it did in movies that took place in boats, or in the staterooms of boats. Mary had always assumed this was artifice, a stagehand's simple replication of the world, and to find it accurate was disturbing to her. She did not want to look at the window, but there were few other places to look. It was a spare room, for all its attempts at grandeur; a blue velvet coverlet on the bed, brass lanterns hanging from brass hooks on the ceiling and the like. It was very early in the evening, only forty minutes since they left the dock. The sun hadn't even gone down, for pity's sake, and yet, here she was, the velvet pressed beneath her buttocks in a way that betrayed the grain of its artificial fur, and Wally pressed above her in a way that betrayed nothing about him. She could see the shoulder of his lavender shirt and the side of his neck, which was corded and sun-burnt. She could see his earlobe and behind it a trim, descending line of brown and gray hair. Wally made no sounds, which she was grateful for. She didn't want to be distracted from her experience of the moment by the experience itself. Wally climbed over her and moved her body as he saw fit. He bent and popped one of her breasts out of the neck of her dress and stuck it in his mouth. It was like being a big padded doll. Mary imagined herself white and jointless. She imagined x's painted in black paint over the spots where Wally might want to suck or press, enter or pinch and the rest of her a vast, pillowy white, a nominal shape meant only to instruct, a teaching tool. The fly buzzed from her lowest abdomen, explored her, absolved her. She was meant, after all, for a purposeful life.

Afterwards, disappointingly, Wally wanted to talk quite a lot. He described the boat to her, its circumference, the depth of its keel. He described afternoons he had spent on the boat, alone but for the subtle crew, trained to anticipate both his desire and his wonder and provide for him an experience he could have achieved on his own only with great forethought and a directed expression of will. He told her that eel grass, "sargassum," Wally corrected himself, traveled across unfathomable distances with its tiny, dependent ecosystem accompanying it from the provisional shelter of its shadow. If one eschewed the Jacuzzi and leaned instead over the railing of the lower deck, one could watch the prow of the yacht break through these floating universes with hardly more than a ripple.

This wasn't to say anything, Wally carefully said. He was stroking her in an assiduous fashion, starting at the hollow of her throat and sliding down her breast and over her stomach, over the peak of her hip and down her leg. It was now outside their moment. He had ought to have let their moment end, and Mary turned crossly on her side and stared at the porthole which was washed with a film of water and salt. Mary imagined the salt all crystallizing very quickly as it might in a movie that used technology to explain the wonders of nature. She imagined the salt building up like a plug over the porthole and making a sound as it grew like the mouth of a bag pulling shut. Wally continued to stroke her side, adjusting to her new position with a break in neither his motion nor narrative.

"I've come to an agreement with myself," Wally said. "I wish other people would intuit that and respect it."

It did not seem to Mary that he was talking to her, but she felt very irritable all of a sudden. The porthole irritated her and also the way the brass lanterns swung out of rhythm with each other, though one might reasonably suppose they were set in motion by the same instigating event. She was irritated with Wally's stroking which was an unthinking action of his hand and not an expression of either mind or will. It was beginning to feel on her skin the way a very cold piece of metal pressed against the sensitive skin of an inner arm or thigh feels like an affront to the spirit rather than the flesh.

"Why don't you just tell them?" Mary said. "Illumine them. Seek clarity." She felt peevish and spiteful. Wally stopped stroking her side but left his hand on her hip, just the tips of his fingers tented on her hip like the legs of a spider suspending its explicit body.

"You little thing," Wally finally said. His tone was amused, but it was clear to Mary that this was now an encounter rather than an affair. The boat heeled and the brass lanterns swayed above them. Wally sat up and buckled his belt. "What are you, do you think?" Wally said. He was musing. Mary rolled over again and considered his profile, watched as he absentmindedly pushed the grain of the velvet back against itself, stroked it smooth. "A fox?" Wally asked, standing and slipping on his shoes. "A mouse? A squirrel?"

That was an interlude, a brief one. Mary was as comfortable with brevity as she was with long, static sprawl. She was actually quite a flexible person, mutable even, agreeable to all sorts of propositions that most people did not have the imagination to proffer. But then the fly began acting up again, buzzing with the kind of fervor she had not felt in years. And then, a few months later, there could be no doubt as to the cause and Charlie was cautiously optimistic, then overjoyed, then settled into the grim wait as she, Mary, walked the long halls of their house in her all-together, requested that their son, now seven, keep out of her sight as much as he could.

Mary did not mention the encounter on the yacht to Charlie. Charlie was doing just fine as he was. When Mary and Wally had ascended from the lower decks, Wally pointing out the finer points in the wood detailing in what Mary wished she could interpret as a cover, Charlie had been dancing with Dina again, or still, a little parody of a jig he was apt to do when he was struggling through, barely making it. He suffered from a lack of competition, was all. He suffered with the warm, sincere suffering of a man who is surrounded by paper cut-outs. Charlie parried and lunged, but even when struck no one around him would condescend to bleed. Really, he was too warm blooded for the world he had been born into. He expected too much affinity from his fellow living creatures, too much regard. They had talked for awhile about getting a pet, some animal to inhabit their living quarters in a fashion wholly unlike the way in which they themselves inhabited the space and thus, instructively, to give Terry an object lesson. To whit: one is not the world but rather one is in it. Additionally: one cannot know, not for sure.

Nothing had ever come of it. They lived in the country, surrounded by acreage in which all manner of animals lived abbreviated lives. Further, they lived not too great a distance from the suburbs where other sorts of animals, those rendered unfit for the forest by a learned capacity to calculate, often went missing and straggled, travel worn and touchingly suspicious, up the slope of their long driveway to lie at the front door. But Terry showed no interest in any of them. Even the box turtles that trundled out from under the hedges to lurch through his elaborate architectural studies, fashioned from rocks and twigs and repurposed swizzle sticks, were greeted with little more than momentary exasperation and gentle relocation. The problem was not that he was a cruel boy. Perhaps there was no problem at all. He was not a child that wanted: not companionship, not accolade. He was a child that existed, often sitting still for long hours on the lawn or in a corner of the house without demonstrable intent or purpose. Terry did not regard his parents or suffer them. He had no need of something to nourish and was frequently misunderstood. Understandably, Mary conceded, Charlie was anxious about how he would react to a sibling.

"He's sensitive," Charlie said. "Too sensitive by far. He'll feel neglected. He'll feel resented."

"He won't," Mary said and inside her the other child, who was maybe a fox or a mouse, who might have the face of an aging man forming in the translucent slosh of its bones, turned in a slow circle.

"Well," Charlie said, "he might feel replaced, then. He's been the only one for so long. He might feel abandoned."

"He won't," Mary said, and turned away from the window where Terry could be seen squatting in near perfect stillness at the base of the forsythia. Every now and then, he would reach out and pat a hummock of mulch, but his attitude was not that of a child immersed in a private fantasy, just as it was neither that of a child waiting nor a child bored. To Mary, he seemed as if he was enacting a prescribed circumlocution. There was room for some variables, but on the whole Terry only did what it was inevitable he should do. He never quite seemed to arrive in a place, say at dinner or at a particular spot in the yard, but it was clear that he traveled. Every moment, so far, her son had spent traveling.

"He'll go on," Mary said. She felt as if she did not know Terry, but she certainly knew of him. She felt as if she had observed him from a great distance and made little annotations regarding his nature every moment of every day since she had returned from the far north and once again taken up the measure of her, and the fly's, life. Perhaps that was mothering, she concluded. It was possible, was it not?, that all along she had been doing it exactly right. Often at night, Mary would go to Terry's bedroom and stand next to the door with her back to the wall. Should he wake up, she would not present to him a looming shadow backlight by the dim ambience of the hallway, but rather only a slightly altered passage in the wall, a shape his eyes would have time to become accustom to before his intellect stirred itself to either acceptance or alarm. This was how she would always like to be with her child, with her children, now; yet Mary knew there were many other ways in which women became mothers. Some of them, like Kris, Mary assumed, placed a series of objects in front of their children and watched intently to see which they would choose. According to that first choice—the fat little hand attracted to the glint of the mirror, the warmth of the coal, the shape of the knife—a series of other objects would be laid in a line. This would guide them in their particular direction, a simulacrum of cause and effect created by the mother as was both her duty and her right.

As a very young woman, Mary might have thought from this model that the mother was a guide bringing the child through life and delivering them to death as a jungle guide might bring a party to a particularly arresting waterfall, or a cave guide to a formation of rocks that looked just exactly like rashers of bacon and sunnyside eggs. However, there was the example of her own mother, a woman who was whittled away by her belief in order and eloquence until she assumed a paradoxically disorderly form, a shape like a root turning in the long darkness, crabbed by rock and clay. But that was such a confusing way of stating things. After all, her mother had only been a woman who died. It was a cancer, one of the usual ones. When alive, her mother had liked certain things, cut flowers, aperitifs, and when she was dead she had ceased to desire any of these things. All the rituals Mary's mother had created in her life came to an untidy end, though her daughter continued to enact them in a painful confused way, returning to certain rooms at certain hours, carrying before her certain objects as if under a spell of her body which compelled her and compelled her though there was no one there to apprehend or acknowledge. Mary's mother had brown hair which she wore cut into a shape that rose from the back of her head like a rising cloud of dust in the road. She had long, intelligent fingers and there was little to be said of her, little time in which to have said it.

Mary herself had grown very thin. The organ in which the child slept rose from her body as if rooted directly in her bones. Her joints articulated themselves with a disturbing fervor. It seemed to Mary as if her son might be awake when she entered his room and stood against his wall. It was something in his stillness, his very still silence, but she said nothing, touched nothing. She was neither the mother who would lay a trail nor the mother who would leave a void. She was the mother who observed. It was not an abnegation of the self so much as it was a reallocation of resources. Her son shifted in bed and made a wet sound with his mouth. Her daughter shifted in her body, perhaps already transfixed by the pull of her brother's gravity, and made no sound.

Mary's other passenger, the fly, was a frantic thing. Its life had been subsumed by a moment of inattention. In spite of the tenacity of her previously held beliefs, the fly held no intent. It was an accident, a happenstance that had ridden in her body all the long years of her life doomed by its belief in its own singular existence, seeking pattern in the fluke rather than escape. The fly buzzed in her throat, but Mary did not choke and, after some time of dry swallowing, she felt it descend to the level of her womb and lost its particular feeling within the feel of her daughter, the long slow dreaming that was happening there. The moon rose over the tree tops and crossed her son's window as small and blind as the eye of a fish long jellied-over on the fisherman's ice.

Mary was tempted to tell all this to the ghost but somehow, whenever the ghost was around, she found herself discussing more topical matters. The ghost did not seem bound by any particular convention, but arrived more readily at mealtimes and was predictable to the point that Mary began to set a place for her at their table. She told Mary that she had been quite a cook in her time. "In my time, for my daughters," the ghost said, "I was known to cook a fish in parchment paper cozened all about with sprigs of dill and tiny baby carrots I would buy at one particular market in spite of the fact that it was out of my way. I made bread from scratch, whipped cream from scratch. You remember how I liked to keep busy, how I liked to fully apprehend my days?"

From comments like these, Mary understood that the ghost was not particularly impressed with the quality of the meals she herself served, but she ate with gusto, helping herself to seconds and lingering at the table long after Charlie and the children had gone off into their private evenings. Mary found herself not ungrateful for the company.

"Is there too much salt in the broth?" Mary asked, her bowl before her and the soup within beginning to skim over with fat.

"Oh no," the ghost replied, dipping her spoon directly into the serving tureen. "If anything, there's too little."

There was never enough salt for the ghost. She often poured a shifting hill of it into her hand in which to dip the tip of her tongue between bites. She changed her clothes an inordinate number of times in a day and appeared to have an endless supply of gauzy scarves which she would tie around the base of her ponytail in order to create a sort of pennant effect, Mary supposed, though they hung limp and passive, doing nothing to mark either changing weather or shifts in the ghosts frequently mercurial moods. The ghost continued not to drink, but she did smoke at an alarming rate. She would often pinch out the end of a half-smoked cigarette and leave it balanced on the edge of an end table or propped against the central stem of a house-plant while she lit another from a bullet shaped silver lighter she was constantly losing in the bottom of her purse. In general, the ghost was a rummager. More than once, Mary caught her dig-ging through the children's drawers, really getting down to the bottom of things, with the clothes themselves stacked in bright piles around her. Though Mary made no special efforts towards stealth, and did not consider herself particularly effected either way by a rearrangement of the children's privacy, the ghost re-acted every time as if they were both trembling on the edge of a social precipice.

"Oh, Mary," the ghost would exclaim, both hands pressed to her chest, cigarette expressing a wavering wreath around her chin. "My dear, it's not how it looks. Let me explain. Do let me make this up with you."

In this scenario, Mary would walk to the window and fiddle with the seam of the curtain. She would look out onto the vantage which sometimes afforded her a view of Terry and Irma, who were seldom apart, and sometimes showed her nothing but the slow affections of the vegetative world: the blades of grass which caressed each other, the banded hostas which yearned, each leaf, away from their tender beds. Not instructive to humans, Mary thought as the ghost shuffled around behind her and continued to protest an innocence that was not in question or of concern. An example of neither the canny nor the marvelous, Mary thought and then she and the ghost would descend the stairs together and the ghost would tell her again some story of her past life which seemed to have been at once full and minutely observed.

Well, Mary supposed, we all have our weaknesses. Her own was a lack of perspective, a new and perplexing inability to keep track of numbers higher than ten. Like a partridge, though her body felt more like the bones of the bird and not its meaty breast, its officious feathers. At night, in bed with Charlie, she described this feeling and he listened in silence. She told Charlie many things and he listened in silence, his back to her and the shape of his body, which had bulked up over the years, soft and dark in the deeper darkness of the room. Sometimes, as she talked, Mary knew the ghost was in the room as well, sitting in the corner of the room in the deep, maroon armchair that was intended for late night vigils though it was seldom used. Sometimes she could hear the ghost somewhere else in the house, the particular weight of her tread, her habit of singing little snatches of song under her breath, and sometimes Mary knew the ghost was gone entirely though where she went when she was not there remained a mystery Mary did not seek to solve.

"My greatest fear has always been too literal a knowledge of myself," Mary told Charlie as they lay together in the dark. "I've overcompensated for that, I know. I've made a mockery of the everyday." Or no. That is not what she said, but what she meant to say. Mary told Charlie stories about her childhood. She told him things her mother had used to say, little snippets, her mother's little habits of speech. She often thought Charlie's naked flesh was like the belly of a toad, porous and impossibly soft, liable to shine with a luminescence entirely independent of light both natural and artificial. Though she had always considered herself to be a rigid woman, pliant in body but never in soul, now Mary wished he would turn over and make a space for her.

"Not to belabor the point," Mary told Charlie, "but I have loved you very much. I have loved you as well as I could." She considered this a transformative moment in their relations with each other. It was some one of a number of very dark nights. The moon in this season seemed disinclined toward illumination, which Mary would have thought a prerequisite of its condition; although, come to think of it, Mary did not even know what the moon was, not for sure. Some kind of orbiting satellite of course, but what of it? What else? She couldn't name even one of the kinds of rocks the moon was composed of or state with any degree of assuredness if it was even composed of rocks and not, perhaps, a very fine, luminous dust compacted into the semblance of a solid, scarred ball. What had been done with all this time she had spent? What had been made of it? The ghost was in the corner sitting in the maroon chair with her knees drawn up to her chest and a musing expression on her face. Mary could not see her, but she knew this was the case. The ghost was on her side, but she had no answers.

"Do you remember the goats?" the ghost said. Her voice in the dark was different than in daylight; a soft and private voice. "Do you remember their dear faces, each one the same face, and the way they would butt their heads up into your palm?"

"I love you, I love you," Mary told Charlie. "I love you. Did you hear me? Did you hear what I said?"

Charlie rolled over. He pulled her against him, put one hand on the side of her face, but it was dark in there, still dark, nothing glowed. Mary could just see the outline of her husband's teeth as he talked. She saw the dark room, dark corners and dark mullion over the window, through the screen of her husband's fingers over her eyes.

"I heard you," said Charlie. "The garden and the river and your friends. The goats and the garden and your friends and the river." Suddenly, she knew. Her husband was not a man, but a grub! He burrowed in the warm earth, turned the soil. Her husband was necessary, but not pleasant to look at. Oh, she had been so mistaken in her life. She had looked in all the wrong places, missed everything.

"Every time you've said something, I've heard it," said Charlie, but of course this was not right.

"This is not then, Mary," said Charlie. "This is here, now. No one else is in this room but us." This was not right either, but closer. The ghost shifted her weight and sighed. She got up and crossed the room. Mary could hear her making her way down the hall toward Irma's room and then, after a brief pause, passing back before their door and down the other end of the hall toward Terry. In the dark house in the long night, the ghost passed from room to room, checking in. Which meant Mary did not have to. Which meant she was not compelled.

"Rot," said Mary. "The soil."

"I know, Mary, I heard you," Charlie said. "The fire, the river, the garden, the goats."

When Mary and Charlie were still in their courting phase they had used to go to a bar out in the country. The bar was called The Silent Woman and it was down a long country road seamed with other roads that leapt out of copses of trees or from between the high cuts of the fields and were always empty. Charlie was a fast driver. He steered with one hand and maneuvered the other back and forth between the gear shift and the radio consol, the rear view mirror, the back of her seat, the top of his head, his mouth. Charlie drove with his whole body, leaning into the curves as they whipped around them, and Mary always felt it would better suit the dramatic narrative of the story if The Silent Woman were at the very end of the road, a beacon gleaming at the head of a cul-de-sac already crowded with other cars into which they could bellow, Charlie announcing their presence by blowing the horn, as the bar's happy patrons spilled out into the parking lot. Instead the bar was just off the road at the edge of a gravel turn-around, unheralded. It was bound on either side by fields which were high with corn or shorn to a copper rubble depending on the season and, while laid perfectly flat to her inspection, always seemed to Mary as if they were full of hidden or merely unperceived lives.

"Sure. Lots of snakes, field mice," Charlie said. Mary felt sure he didn't know any more about these things than she did, but when he drove his fingers raked through his hair or came to rest in the center of his lower lip and seemed imbued with a private temperament at which Mary could not stop looking. Charlie did not look at her. He shifted gears. He stamped the clutch flat to the mat and let it out by begrudging inches while Mary had a little flask with her initials etched in silver spirals on the front which Charlie had given her and which he thoughtfully filled for her so she would have something to do on the ride.

Outside the bar was a sign that showed the bar's name, but did not spell it out. The sign depicted a woman in an ankle length blue dress. She was wearing a long white apron and carrying a silver tray with a single silver cup set upon it which, by the careful way she gripped either side of the tray, was probably full. The woman had a wide, soft, white collar and above that nothing—no head, no hair, no habits of expression. She was the silent woman and Mary was taken with her and thought about her as she and Charlie sat at a wobbly table and watched the people at the bar dance, waved for the waitress to come bring them more drinks and, eventually, danced themselves amid the crush of bodies. The band throbbed in the corner and Charlie's hands were damp on Mary's hip and buttocks. Mary twirled around and around, her head bobbing over Charlie's shoulder.

"What kind of shoes was she wearing?" Mary would shout, pressing a thumb against the base of Charlie's ear so he would hear her. "It's a test. What kind of ring did she have on her right index finger?" Charlie spun her around and around while the band played. The bar was always packed.

One day, they drove out to The Silent Woman. Charlie had not yet proposed but Mary knew it was a matter of time.

"A waiting game," her father had said. "He's a man who needs time to see what he thinks." Mary's father was not entirely sold on Charlie. He had not been entirely won over by Charlie's satellite courtship of him which had involved gifts of liquor and cigars and, once, a book bound in brown leather which showed the inside view of all the different kinds of ships built in the harbor in the early days of the city's preeminence. Mary thought the book was interesting in a terrible way—all those ships splayed open, gaping, the tiny kegs of rum or salted fish stowed away by tiny sailors who clambered through the ship's holds oblivious to the ruin of the shape that was to keep them safe on open seas. But her father was not given to flights of fancy and remained impervious to Charlie's advances. Her father, in his encroaching age, had shut up like a clam shell. He was not waiting for anything anymore and his modes of locomotion became mysterious, seldom glimpsed. In fact, Mary's father was starting to become a problem for her, but now, in Charlie's car, going fast down a straight road with Charlie's hand on the back of her seat and his arm stretched taught between them, she considered herself problem free. So many things were meant to be left behind. It was impossible for any one person, and certainly not for her, a motherless child, little more than a girl despite her tight, short skirt, to have too explicit a say in what was lost and what was gained.

Charlie was in a fine mood. He sang along to the radio and occasionally lifted his hand up to her face, holding his fist like a microphone she should sing into as well, though she did little more than lean forward and breathe. The moon was out. That was something Mary would always later remember. The moon was fat and low and orange as a persimmon. It seemed to be traveling along the horizon line like an animal preoccupied with marking its own progress. The moon traveled back and forth along the horizon line snuffling in the underbrush. It was fall. The air was high and sharp and they traveled down the road quickly in a straight line.

"The stars are so far away," Charlie sang. It was a line from a children's song which someone had redone with electric guitars and heavy drums. Mary didn't even know how he had found that station on the radio. He held his hand up to her face and Mary breathed into it, imagining her breath seeping down between the creases of his hands and condensing there, a damp ball rapidly cooling.

"They never speak when spoken to," Charlie sang.

That night, the bar was more than usually full. Mary and Charlie had to share their table with another couple, slightly younger than them, who looked alike with a burnished, simple similitude Mary found soothing. The boy was tall with unusually long hair which he wore loose over his shoulders and there was something about his teeth, something about his teeth behind his cheeks, that was very apparent. The girl was smaller and plainer. She seemed to huddle into herself the way a bird or a small mammal will huddle into its down or fur for comfort and protection from the cold, but, Mary noticed, it was the boy who sought reassurance. He couldn't keep his hands off her. Always touching the back of her hand, stroking her knee, circling her wrist with his thumb and index finger as if making her a bracelet and then trying it on for fit. They were both absorbed in the music, jogging their knees under the table to the beat.

"What a beautiful couple," Mary said to Charlie. He gave her a squeeze, but was mostly preoccupied trying to get the waitress's attention. He thrust his hand into the air and waved it back and forth in an exaggerated fashion that reminded Mary of semaphore. The ancient sea language for two rye whiskeys, neat, she thought and laughed. The girl caught her eye and smiled with her, though she could not possibly get the joke. That was the kind of people she needed, Mary thought. People who were pleased to be in the here and now; people who were gracious about it. The band swung into another song without pausing for breath.

It seemed to Mary as if this night had been traveling toward her for a long time. Their drinks arrived and she sipped hers, the liquor sliding down her throat in an obedient fashion, all as expected. It seemed to Mary as if she had seen this before, which of course she had, many times over the months she and Charlie had been dating, but tonight something was the same in a very particular way. Mary let herself wander out over the crowd. In her physical body she was sitting with her back to the wall, Charlie's hand on her thigh like a lap rug. The young couple got up and moved to the dance floor where they began some kind of mirror dance, the girl leading and the boy copying her movements with a sinuous intent. Mary took another sip of her drink and moved in her non-physical self out between the tables and the crowed, rickety chairs, past the drinkers who were laughing or nodding intently or drawn and pale and alone, past the black and chrome dental chair at the corner of the bar which was reserved for the owner, an elderly man with a menacing haircut who was often hobbled with the gout, and over to the dance floor where she slipped between the couples, feeling the push and pull of their bodies like the tide tormenting a water weed.

She drifted around on the bandstand for awhile. The drummer was admirably out of place. Too tall and thin and pale for his position in the band, nevertheless, he pounded a complicated rhythm and rocked back and forth in his seat with his eyes shut, the color progressively draining from his face. He seemed about to collapse, but Mary understood from the angle of his torso as he leaned away from the noise he was making that this was a choice, this calamitous solitude he had created at the back of the band. The other band members were hardly better off. There was a guitarist and a singer and a trumpet player. They were in the middle of a long, complicated instrumental solo, and the singer seemed at a bit of a loss. He had loose limbs which appeared to have too many joints and jangled a tambourine against the side of his long haunch in such a way that suggested that even if the instrument were not there he would be making the same discordant noise. He had long, yellow teeth which showed to great advantage as he blurted counterpoint sounds into the microphone. The guitarist was smoking, smoke fanning back from the cigarette and making his eyes blink and water.

The dancers were really getting into it. Everyone in the bar seemed to feel the eternal weight of the now in the same way Mary felt it. They were of accord. Certainly the dancers were not all beautiful people, but to Mary, traveling through them with the freedom of a woman released from her body, released by Charlie's satisfaction with the scene from the need to nod and smile, to hold his hand as it rested atop her thigh smothering the flesh beneath it in a wide, wet shape the same shape as his palm, they seemed to scintillate. All the people in the room gathered light within themselves and sent it flashing back. Every person in the room refracted from many internal facets.

There were four women on the dance floor who seemed to have come with the same man. The women had an affinity, sisters perhaps, and were wearing variations of the same checked dress from whose old fashioned lace collars their necks rose columnar and surprisingly thick. Each woman had fixed her hair in the same way as the others, two loose plaits that started at the crown of their heads and flopped over their ears as they danced, and they each possessed the same wide, tawny eyes. The one in the pink and white check was the prettiest, somehow. She held each of her sisters' hands in turn, encouraging them, bringing them further into themselves. The man they came with was short and fiery. He was an antonym to the sisters' willowy limbs and paunchy torsos, and wore a trim black suit with a stiff white shirt and a skinny black tie. His hair was white and rose from his head a bristling inch before subsiding angrily down the back of his neck. Oh, how he stomped and pawed! He described a furious circle around the sisters and they turned to follow his progress, eyes placid, a little wicked, unblinking. The sisters all had small hands and small precise feet. They had prominent hipbones and Mary understood they were women who were afraid only of the elements. Nothing less could sway them. Nothing less could make them blanch.

How strange that I am in this place and not some one of the many other places I have been, Mary thought. It was one of those thoughts that seemed to be spoken by someone else, an overheard thought. She could see the waitress, Joellen or Joanne or some other name she could never quite remember, behind the bar filling an order that was probably their second round. Joellen speared a cherry with a blue cocktail sword and slid it all the way to the sword's hilt. She speared another.

Mary looked across the room and saw herself leaning back against the wall. She was so young, so comely. On her face there was a look of perfect, removed expectation. Something was coming to her, all right, and her hand on the table, Mary's very own hand there on the table, followed the high notes of the trumpet just now starting in with a fluidity she had not known she possessed. Charlie shifted in his seat so he could look at the side of her face, surreptitiously. Across the room, of course, Mary could see it all, but the Mary right next to him was as unaware as if she were made of cold wax, an unlit taper, full of potential. Somebody strike the fucking spark, Mary thought and she watched the thought blaze up in her face and turn her cheeks pink. Her lips parted. She stared out over the crowd, seeing nothing, and Charlie was so hungry; he was ravenous. He leaned toward her, his cheeks hollow with hunger, and she knew in a moment he would pull her to him, turn her head toward him and they would meet at the mouth and eat from each other and be filled.

"Strike the spark!" Mary said.

Joellen brought them their drinks and set them down hastily, slopping them onto the table. She had her hands full. She was practically running with that long gliding stride that comes from voluntary servitude, a sense of self that can be put on hold. Some of the men were excited by this and reached out after her to slide their hands across the shiny seat of her pants, pinch the soft white flesh that bloomed under the fabric just below her back pocket. Mary took a sip of her drink and Mary watched herself swallow. She lifted the cocktail sword from the glass and slid the cherry off between her teeth. Charlie was leaning closer. There was something different about the shape of his head, something she couldn't remember having seen before, but perhaps it was that they were so young, so in love. Joellen was okay; she was moving very fast. She hoisted a tray onto her shoulder and walked through the crowd with the full drinks chiming next to her ear. She was a statue rising above the surf. The men's hands rose up after her, red and cramped like the little claws of a crawfish, boiled open. The trumpeter played and played and played her repetitive song. She inserted herself, irrevocably, into the scene.

Both Marys turned to watch her. Both Marys felt a surge of jealously at the way her body filled her black cat suit at the hips and breast. Both Marys admired her shining hair and strong jaw line, her small ears and the way her eyes focused on the bell of her horn and no further, took nothing else into account. Both Marys closed their eyes. The trumpet was astonishingly loud. The room was very hot. Heat filled the room as if it were pouring through a crack in the ceiling and running down the wall in rills. A blast of heat blew across her cheeks and nose, across her eyelids. Someone put their hand on Mary's chin and turned her head. Someone pressed their mouth against Mary's mouth and when they pulled away she sat with her mouth open as the band shook all manner of things loose from the rafters, as the drinkers swept through the door headless of what drafted in after them. She caught her breath; she swallowed. The trumpet blatted triumphantly. The drums banged.

"The stars are too many to count," said the singer. He was breaking in. It wasn't quite his turn. "The stars are so far away."

"They're playing our song," said Charlie. Mary could feel a strand of saliva strung between his lip and hers. She opened her eyes and saw his face from so close it was like nothing else she had ever seen or ever would. It was his face but looked like the great, shocked face of the moon and, also like the moon, it was orange in the weird bar light. Around them, there was a tumult and the strange jangle of the tambourine sounded more and more like crackling, a rising din.

"Why is it so hot in here?" Mary said, but no one answered. She coughed. She swallowed something like a little pill and felt its rough edges scratch all the way down her throat.

Mary was asleep. She was having a dream. In the dream, the ghost was telling her a long story with some urgency.

"Listen," said the ghost. "I met him in the garden."

Mary looked around to see if she was in the garden again. She regretted ever having been so unguarded with the place. She also regretted the regret, but there it was. Some things cannot be passed off as a folly of youth; sometimes a permanent damage has been done.

But no, Mary wasn't in the garden, not anywhere near it. She was in her own room, in her own bed, just as she had entered it the night before and brought the covers up over her shoulder thinking, I will never get to sleep at this rate, until suddenly she was asleep and having this dream. By the slant of the light and the empty hanger on the closet doorknob which had held Charlie's suit coat the previous night, she surmised the time in the dream was late morning. In the dream, she had overslept.

"This is unlike me," Mary said. She propped the pillows under her back and sat up against the headboard. Outside the window, a large brown bird was in the spruce, hopping from limb to limb. It wasn't looking in the window exactly, but it clearly knew the window was there. Its entire affect betrayed its awareness of the window. For the life of her, Mary couldn't think what it could want.

The ghost was sitting at the foot of the bed, practically on top of Mary's feet. She looked terrible, her hair disheveled, her salmon pink blouse stained and misbuttoned. She looked into the air with a vacant remembered expression that Mary found annoying.

"I intended nothing. That was a time in my life when I had no intent but a kind of expulsion instead. Sort of like how a squid swims around in the upper levels of the ocean by pulling water into its body and then expelling the water in a jet? I guess you could say I had propulsion, and of course that heightened sex drive." The ghost laughed. She was suddenly right there with Mary, beaming into Mary's face. The ghost gripped Mary's toes beneath the blankets and shook them. There was a joke to be shared and the ghost was sharing it. She had always been that sort of woman, Mary thought. Afraid to be alone.

"Was I there, too?" Mary asked. It seemed a reasonable question. After all, she had been so often in the garden, so often with her friends sitting around the picnic table under the trellis passing glasses back and forth while the garden grew still and gray and then flared silver with the rising moon. Sometimes, light would fall across the sky and it was impossible to tell whether it was a shooting star or a satellite. Whether it crossed the sky with intent or hapless abandon. "Was Donovan there? Or August?"

But the ghost ignored her. She might as well have said nothing at all. The ghost crawled up the bed on all fours and lay down beside Mary. She tucked herself around Mary's body and stroked the side of Mary's face as she talked.

"His first name was Mark, did you know that?, and I asked him what his middle name was, but that was some kind of breach of privacy with him, one step too far, although of course, we had already gone way too far and we both knew it. I wasn't stupid, Mary, and nobody thought I was but you, poor dear." The ghost traced Mary's hairline, rubbed her earlobe between her fingers. She scratched the soft swag of skin just below Mary's chin the way one would a cat or small dog whose humor one was trying to cultivate.

"Anyway, he stripped me out of my clothes like that." The ghost snapped her fingers and held them up in the air before her face as if she were seeing the sound. "But he was still in his suit, you know that grey one he wore even though everyone else was so casual?, and when he knelt down he got big wet stains on his knees and I remember thinking that would be a hard thing to explain if anyone came across him later, although it wouldn't be, of course. He could just say he dropped his keys and had to pat around to find them. He could have said anything at all and no one would have questioned."

Mary tried to picture the garden: its doddering phlox, its heady scents. She tried to picture the river and feel again the precise place on her shin where it had reached its highest tide, rilled and receded. She felt as if something were being taken from her. Each word that came out of the ghost's mouth took another word away from Mary which she would never again be able to use. The bird hopped onto the windowsill and cocked its head as if asking a question, but that was all anthropomorphic nonsense. That was all a fantasy of the self projected onto the wholly unconcerned itdom of the bird. Mary was disgusted with herself. She detected a faint smell, like the faintest whiff of decay when one is still far down the beach and has not come upon the source bloating in the tide, and knew it was emanating from somewhere within her own person. The garden was lost to her. She could not imagine it. She could not reinhabit its space.

"But that's not what I'm telling you about, Mary," said the ghost. She smacked her palm against Mary's stomach, and then against the tops of each of her thighs. The ghost was very close to her ear, talking directly into Mary's ear so she both heard and felt her words. "That's not what I'm talking about at all." The ghost stuck her tongue into Mary's ear; she took Mary's earlobe gently between her teeth.

"Listen," said the ghost, "when Dumma was born she didn't breathe at all for the first three minutes. She slid out of me like a pip from an orange. She was so self-contained and quiet and the most beautiful color. I really can't tell you how beautiful a color Dumma was, just this pale, uncomplicated blue. Anyway, the nurses whisked her right up, you can imagine, and carried her away to the corner where they bent over her and said tight, grim things and everyone started to move in this very constricted sort of way, like their joints had frozen up?, which I understood was the motion of emergency, but I wasn't worried. I wasn't even upset. I remember thinking, well, at least this one will be easy. Because her sister was such a spitfire, and because I had already been tired so often in my life. Do you know that way you get tired that you can't ever recover from? Well, I was that way when I was only ten. I just wasn't born with any resiliency. I was born already partially used up." The ghost shifted around on the bed so she was lying on top of Mary. She lined her arms up with Mary's arms and her legs with Mary's legs. She spoke directly into Mary's mouth. The bird suddenly, savagely, attacked the glass with its beak.

"Finally, I spoke up," the ghost said into Mary's mouth. "Can you imagine the scene? Me in bed, flattened really, all the vessels in my eyes broken open, still leaking, and all those official sorts of people clustered at the other end of the room, bent over that little wax doll like she was the first brand new thing they had ever seen? Well, it was disgusting, let me tell you that. I said, pretty loudly if I recall, I said, 'Leave her alone!' I said, 'Leave her be!'" The ghost's breath was overly sweet, like the breath of a flower bloomed past its peak, unpollenated. Somehow Mary couldn't see the ghost's face, though it was so close. Somehow Mary couldn't move.

"They ignored me of course, they always do, but that was the first time I ever stood up for my daughter and it was at no small personal cost. I meant Dumma could choose what she wanted. I meant Dumma could just as easily never have taken a breath at all and it wouldn't have invalidated her as an object of worth." The bird flung itself against the glass, making an unrelenting noise. It battered the glass with its wings, struck at it with its claws. The expression in the bird's eyes had not changed at all. There was no expression in the bird's eyes, Mary thought, that was what had not changed. Nothing.

"Then, of course, Dumma took a big breath, all on her own, and started to wail. I felt so betrayed, Mary. I felt, for the first time, like I really understood just how unconcerned with a person's feelings the world could be." The ghost was quiet, but she kept breathing. Her breath flowed over Mary, into Mary. Together they listened as the bird broke its beak on the glass—the thin noises it made, a cry hurking out of its broken face unlike song or anything else.

"When we left the garden I could already smell smoke," said the ghost. "I remember saying as I zipped up my jeans, 'Is someone burning leaves?' and I remember him saying, quite distinctly, 'I'm sure it's nothing,' and walking away." The ghost pressed her lips against Mary's lips and when she spoke Mary's lips moved with the words. Deep in her stomach something shifted, a furtive tingling and then, unmistakable, a buzz.

"Of course it was nothing," the ghost and Mary said. Up her esophagus, over its ribbed tubing and slick red muscle, past the tonsils and the epiglottis, at the root of her tongue, at the back of her teeth, the sticky feet and bristling chest, the buzz, the buzz, the wings long stiff, now limbering. On the tip of her tongue, the million facets of its eyes finally refracted light. "Not yet, at least," the ghost and Mary said. The fly perched for the briefest of moments on Mary's lower lip. It rubbed its forelegs together, tested its wings. "At the moment," they said, "it was nothing at all."

The bird, or something else, began to wail. Its noise spilled out of it and racketed around the room. Something else was said, but no one could tell what it was. There was a pervasive sense of lethargy, of weight. There was a lurch and then another. The room steeled itself to stillness and the dream it had been having of itself flared and went out.

Later, Irma came in. Mary was sitting in the maroon chair, the ghost perched beside her, balancing on the chair's arm. Irma had been at school and was still wearing her school uniform which, Mary saw, was too small for her, too tight at the waist, flaring over her buttocks in an odd shape like the bell of an umbrella. Otherwise, she looked fine. She had beautiful skin, truly lucent skin, and long brown hair which she wore bound up at the nape of her neck in a style that was much too old for her. Irma looked just like her brother and they both looked just like Charlie. Mary could see nothing of herself in Irma's face and for that, among other things, she loved her very much.

Irma walked past Mary and the ghost and stood by the side of the bed. "Mom?" she said, but she had it wrong. Mary wasn't what was in the bed anymore; she had left all that behind her. Mary was over here, in the chair, by the window. She sighed in exasperation. Children got everything wrong the first time. It was like a game for them, but they played it so seriously it was tedious for everyone else involved. The ghost had tidied herself up considerably, rebuttoned her blouse, done something with her hair. What was in the bed was lying there in the most slovenly way. Its mouth was open. Everything else in the room was closed: all the doors, all the windows. The air was heavy, cloying and the only sign left of the bird was a tiny comet of blood arcing across a lower plane.

"Otherwise, everything is just as I left it," Mary said.

"Well, that's an accomplishment, I suppose," said the ghost. Mary didn't like her tone, but she supposed they had all been under a great deal of stress. A long journey had been taken, and at the end of it they were both still here, no closer to illumination.

"Mom?" said Irma. She reached out and put her hand over the hand of what was in the bed. She already knew, that much was clear. Irma had already known for all of her life, but what could she do? She was a child, at the most hideous of disadvantages. Mary considered that she was handling herself quite well if all the factors were taken into account.

"What happens next?" said Mary, but the ghost was not listening to her. She swung her leg back and forth as if enjoying the motion of the joint and hummed a little song under her breath. Outside the trees tossed back and forth in a breeze that had been circling the world for some time, gaining and losing strength. That breeze had crested off the top of a pyramid, got caught up in the spume from a whale's blowhole. It had been chopped to pieces by a plane's propeller but reassembled itself and moved on. Soon enough, it was gone and no one had answered Mary's question. No one had answered Irma's question. No one had said anything at all.

Mary watched as her daughter lifted the hand and pressed it against her cheek. She watched as her daughter climbed into the bed and tucked herself under the arm attached to the hand, adjusted the fit until she was wholly contained within an embrace. Irma's lips were artificially pink as if she had been eating something she probably should not. Her eyes were as glossy as buttons. The moment continued for a long time and then another one came along and replaced it.

Acknowledgments

My grateful thanks to the editors at whose journals the following stories were previously published:

"Listen," *New Orleans Review*

"A Category of Glamour," *The Burnside Review*

"A Terrible Thing," *Web Conjunctions*

"The Cherry Tree," *American Fiction*

"A Beautiful Girl, A Well Loved One," *Fairy Tale Review*

"The Dinner Party," *Alaska Quarterly Review*

"Mother Box," *Conjunctions*

"Conversation," *Western Humanities Review*

Deepest thanks also to: the University of Alabama MFA program, particularly Kate Bernheimer, Michael Martone, Joel Brouwer and Wendy Rawlings: for the beginnings, the middles, and the ends. To Lance Olson, Dan Waterman, Noy Holland and all the other editors, copyeditors and readers at FC2 and University of Alabama

Press who have helped this book on its way to print. To Dr. Roy Fluhrer and the Fine Arts Center for the time and the Vermont Studio Center for the space. To Mike Stutzman, Jillian Weise, Carl Peterson, Rachel Mack, Molly Dowd, Laura Hendricks Ezell, Tim Croft, Bard Cole and Alissa Nutting: first readers, dear friends. To my sister, Katie Blackman, first friend.

To my father for his philosophy of kindness. To my mother for her philosophy of happiness.

To John Pursley III who knows my heart. To Helen Maria Pursley who owns my heart.

Notes

The Joy Williams epigram is taken from her book, *The Changeling*, reissued by Fairy Tale Review Press in 2008.

The line "Time to make more cats," in the story "Listen," is taken from Louise Gluck's poem, "After the Storm," originally published in *The New Yorker*.

The title of "A White Hat on his Head, Two Wooden Legs," is taken from a Welsh children's song called "I Saw a Jackdaw," which is about just that.

The lines that Charlie and the singer in the band sing in "The Silent Woman," are from the children's poem "Stars" by Charles Sandberg.

In the same story, the image of a headless woman serving drinks is borrowed from the signs of various pubs and bars called either

The Silent Woman or The Good Woman which are spread across the United Kingdom. I owe the discovery of this image to my good friend the poet Mike Stuzman who thought I would think it was funny.